THREE-MAN ADVANTAGE

TRIPPING - BOOK 2

ARIEL BISHOP

For Alex and Brittany
I love you

CONTINENTAL HOCKEY LEAGUE

New England Division

Baltimore Basilisks

Providence Griffins

Boston Banshees

New York Gargoyles

New Jersey Reapers

Toronto Trolls

Ottawa Sirens

Montreal Manticores

Seaboard Division

Carolina Chimeras
Miami Hellhounds
Pensacola Hydras
Philadelphia Phantoms
Washington Wyverns
Atlanta Krakens
Nashville Nagas
Kansas City Centaurs

Heartland Division

Wisconsin Wendigos
Texas Thunderbirds
Chicago Wizards
New Mexico Jackalopes
Detroit Sphinxes
Colorado Yetis
Alberta Abominables
Montana Werewolves

Gold Coast Division

Seattle Selkies
Vegas Vampires
Portland Sasquatches

Arizona Phoenixes

Los Angeles Chupacabras

San Jose Dragons

Idaho Giants

Vancouver Leviathans

WISCONSIN WENDIGOS LINEUP

Forwards

First Line

Xander "Richie" Richards - Left

David "Sonny" Dickson - Center (C)

Agustin "Becks" Zubeck

Second Line

Chan "Singer" Hsing - Left

Josh "Harty" Hartsburg - Center

Andrew "Molly" Yermolayev - Right

Third Line

Adam "Huffs" Hufford - Left

Arthur "Shinny" Mishin - Center

Paul "Deelio" Deel - Right

Fourth Line

Daniel "Yo" Portillo - Left
Roger "Haircut" Barbour - Center
Jamie "Parks" Parker - Right
Fifth Line
Timothy "Annie" Scanian - Left
Jeffrey "Beans" Rice - Center
Tony "Mary" Mariano - Right

Defense

First Pair
Aleksandr "Sasha" Ivanov (A)
Dalton "Elvis - Presby
Second Pair
Samir "Dino" Medina
Rodion "Niki" Kolesnikov
Third Pair
Patrick "Ake" Akesson
Ian "Danny" McDaniel
Fourth Pair
Ron "Silver" Silvey
Ivan "Rosie" Rosario

Goalies

Bo "Mac" MacAllister (A)

Henrik "Ricky" Pohjonen
Lucas "LK" King

Utility

Adriano "Ads" Cruz (D)
Oscar "Baldy" Baldwin (F)
Seth "Con" Connolly (F)
Liam "Mal" Malbrough (D)
Aiden "Ray" Reynolds (F)
Mitchell "Jacks" Jackson (F)

DAVID

"Hey, Cap."

David looks up from unlacing his skates at the familiar voice. Sasha must have taken advantage of David staying behind to help Ray with his backhand. He's freshly showered, long hair hair damp and curling slightly behind his ears and at the nape of his neck, stray water droplets clinging to his bare chest—David tears his eyes away.

By now he should be used to Sasha's habit of wandering around the locker room wearing only a very small towel, if that. It's not like he's the only one—at least half the Wendigos are shameless nudists, and it seems to get worse with every new crop of rookies. But with most of them, David has no trouble looking away. Yes, hockey creates attractive bodies, but there are only two cases where David feels the magnetic pull, the need to stare. One of them is Sasha.

"Hey," he says back, returning his attention to the laces he's somehow managed to knot together, trying to ignore Sasha's muscular thighs in his peripheral vision. "What's up?"

"Bo says I should talk to you about party," Sasha says, settling down on the bench next to him. "How we can help, all that."

The stubborn laces finally come apart, and David shucks his skates off before starting on the rest of his gear. It's stupid to feel shy about it, but between Sasha sitting so close and Mac watching from the goalie stall at the end, he feels caught, self-conscious in a way he hasn't since his first Juniors locker room. And not just because Sasha always calls Mac by his actual name, a small intimacy he tries not to think too hard about.

"The Thanksgiving party, right," he answers eventually, voice muffled as he pulls the practice jersey off over his head, holding up a hand when he sees Con's mouth open all the way across the room. "I know, Connolly, I know, American Thanksgiving."

"I'm just saying," Con mutters, loud enough to be heard out on the ice, as usual.

David can't help grinning, the normalcy of the exchange helping him feel more settled in his skin. "Tell you what, Con, you convince the CHL to make Canadian Thanksgiving an official holiday and we'll do two parties. But until then, we're in Wisconsin, so suck it up and be thankful we're not actually playing that day, for once."

"Amen," Dino chimes in as he heads out the door. "Make sure you have pumpkin pie, Cap."

"You'll eat what we have and you'll like it," David calls after him.

Sasha laughs quietly next to him. "So, you have plan? Or we need make plan?"

"I have—part of a plan," David admits. "We should probably sit down and go over it, but I'm gonna hit the showers first. I stink."

He realizes his mistake when Sasha leans in even closer, the tip of his nose just barely brushing David's neck, and inhales. "Smell fine to me," Sasha murmurs, a barely audible rumble compared to his usual booming voice. "But go, keep Bo company."

David is too busy trying to escape before Sasha notices his reaction to parse that last statement until he makes it into the showers, empty except for Mac. Of fucking course.

"Hey, Cap." Mac turns his back to the spray, closing his eyes as he tips his head back to wet his hair, plastering the dark shock of it to his skull. "Sash and I were thinking lunch? We can go over the party plans and stuff our faces at the same time."

"Sounds good." David hopes his voice isn't as choked as it sounds in his own ears, but the universe is clearly conspiring against him. Going from Sasha's half-naked proximity to this, water cascading down over Mac's compactly muscled chest—fuck. "What were you guys thinking? Sushi?"

Mac shrugs, opening his eyes and reaching for the soap. "Works for me. I'll check with Sash when I get back out there. You want to ride with us?"

"I can meet you," David says, doing his best to concentrate on cleaning himself off and not the lazy movements of Mac's hands over his torso, sliding down into dangerous territory before David manages to tear his eyes away. The last thing he needs when he's this on edge is to be crammed into the middle seat of Mac's ridiculous pickup truck. "I have some errands I need to run after."

"Whatever works."

Mac steps out from under the spray, grabbing a towel and scrubbing it over his hair and body for fucking ever before wrapping it loosely around his waist and disappearing in the direction of the locker room.

David slumps against the wall for a second, just breathing. The locker room showers aren't the ideal place to give himself a pep talk, but it looks like this is where it needs to happen.

You are an adult man, he tells himself, reaching for the soap and scrubbing over his skin with impatient motions. *You are going to go have lunch with your alternate captains who are also your best friends. You are going to plan the best Thanksgiving party this team has ever seen. You will not ogle them or get lost in thought trying to figure out if they're actually together or just really good friends. Then you will go home, take your nap, come back here, and play some damn good hockey.*

He thinks darkly, as he dries himself off and heads back into the locker room to get dressed, that this is all Xander's fault. Ever since he started dating Jordan, the team's massage therapist, he's been gently poking at David, trying to get him to make a move.

Which is just ridiculous. The pool on whether or not Mac and Sasha are together has never actually been won. Either they're very good at keeping things under wraps, or there's nothing going on.

But even if they are together, there's no reason to think that they, what, would welcome David in? That's not—normal people don't do that.

David has long ago resigned himself to the stupidity of being attracted to both of his alternate captains. But he's not willing to risk the humiliation of opening himself up to rejection from two people at the same time. He may play hockey, but that doesn't make him a masochist.

His phone vibrating in his bag pulls him out of the all-to-familiar depressing spiral. It takes a few seconds of squinting at the calendar reminder before it makes sense, but then the pieces come together in his head. He pulls his shirt over his head, unlocks his phone and scrolls through the contacts until he finds the right one. A quick pause to put on his socks and shoes and then he hits the call button, tying his shoes with the phone held between his ear and his shoulder as it rings.

Aunt Kathy picks up on the third ring. "David! What a nice surprise!"

"You know I wouldn't miss your birthday," he

replies, thanking his past self once again for taking the time to set up calendar reminders for this kind of shit. "Not for my favorite aunt."

"Boy, you better be careful spreading that bullshit around," she says, laughing. "You think I don't know how you are?"

He smiles. "It's not bullshit if it's the truth, Aunt Kathy."

She snorts a little when she laughs, just like she always does, and for a moment he's ten again, chasing his cousins around her backyard while Mama and the aunts sit on the patio talking about grown-up things, Daddy and the uncles gathered around the grill doing the same. "Whatever you say, boy. How're you doing out there? They treating you alright? Your mama says you're having a real good season."

"We're doing our best," David says, trying to think of a safe topic to keep things from dissolving into awkward silence. "How's Chris and Brittany's baby doing?"

Fortunately that sets her off on a good fifteen-minute spiel about the perfection of her newest grandchild, barely pausing for breath. All he has to do is say "uh-huh" and "wow, really" at intervals.

"I'm gonna have to go, Aunt Kathy," he finally

says once she temporarily runs out of things to talk about. "I have a lunch meeting for team stuff and I'll be late if I don't get going."

"You work too hard," she says, her voice fond. "When are you gonna find a nice girl or boy to settle down with? You know your mama would love some grandbabies."

David winces, grateful that she can't seen his face. "Maybe someday. But I'd hate to have a kid and not see them half the year because of hockey."

"Other people make it work," she persists. "I don't like thinking about you out there in Milwaukee all by yourself."

"I have my team," David says reflexively. "Honestly, it's hard to be all by myself; there's always somebody around. I promise I'm okay, Aunt Kathy."

She sighs, and he can picture the expression on her face clearly. "Whatever you say, boy. But you'd better come see me when you come visit your parents this summer, you hear?"

"Cross my heart," he promises, and manages to extricate himself from the call with only a couple more minutes of small talk.

And if he feels a little out of sorts on the drive to the restaurant, it's because talking to Aunt Kathy made him feel homesick. He's not lonely. There's always someone around.

He's fine.

"So," Mac says once they're settled into a corner booth at Midori, drinks and sushi ordered. "Thanksgiving. What's the plan?"

"Right." David closes his eyes for a second, trying to school his thoughts into some kind of order and stop wallowing in stupid feelings. "First off, we need to get a final head count of who's going to be there and who isn't."

Sasha nods, his shoulder brushing against Mac's. "Richie say he's going home with Jordy, meet his Nana."

They share a moment of silence as they all try to picture how that will go. Or maybe that's just David.

"Good luck to him," Mac says after a minute. "Anybody else that we know of?"

It turns out that the number of guys on the team going home for Thanksgiving is surprisingly small. Or maybe not that surprisingly; they may not have a game on Thanksgiving day, but they have a back-to-back Friday and Saturday and none of them want to be dealing with jet lag for that.

"Okay," David says once they've double-checked their list, added significant others and children. "So I'll order the catering—"

"You not going to cook for us?" Sasha mock pouts.

Mac smacks him lightly on the arm. "Trust me, we're all better off with the caterer."

"Hey," David objects. "I'm not that bad."

"Cap, did you or did you not manage to fuck up Kraft Dinner?" Mac asks, eyes twinkling as Sasha laughs.

David rolls his eyes. "That was one fucking time. But we're gonna have like forty people; I'm not going to kill myself making that much food."

"Good plan," Sasha approves, patting him on the shoulder with one big hand. "What we do?"

"You two are in charge of pie," David says, doing his best to ignore the way his heart races a little at the touch—what is he, a fucking teenager? "Call that bakery today, the good one one, before they stop taking Thanksgiving orders."

Mac shoots him a lazy salute. "Yes, sir. Anything else?"

They pause for a moment as the waitress stops

by their table with a tray full of food. There's only just enough room for everything they ordered, two rolls apiece and a couple of orders of gyoza in the middle.

"Oh, drinks!" David says once she's left again, unwrapping his chopsticks. "Figure out how much beer we need. And wine or whatever. Just not too much of the hard stuff; the last thing I need is the rookies doing tequila shots in my house."

"Vodka shots okay?" Sasha asks with a grin. "Maybe Jello?"

David glares at him, but it has just as much effect as it always does, which is to say, none. "If you get Jello shots on my carpet, Alexsandr Dmitriyevich Ivanov, we are going to have words."

"Oooh," Mac sing-songs. "Real name and everything. You're in trouble."

"That goes for you too, Bo," David says, transferring his glare to Mac, where it's equally effective. "This is going to be a family event. Let's try to keep the drunkenness to a minimum. Until the kids go home, at least."

Sasha nods. "Understand. No shots until kids gone."

David turns his attention back to his food. It seems like the better part of valor, at least when the alternative is watching Mac eat sushi with his hands, licking the sauce off his fingertips. Or, fuck David's entire life, offering Sasha a bite, smiling when Sasha's mouth closes over his fingers.

"Anything else?" Mac asks, turning back toward David like he hadn't been making googly-eyes at his probably-boyfriend. "Hey, you should try some of this, Cap. The crab is amazing."

He picks up another slice before David can protest, leaning closer to offer it. David should say no, should return to his own food, should at the very least take it out of Mac's hand before eating it.

But apparently today is not a day for good decisions, because what he actually does is lean in just like Sasha did. The crab is delicious, just as promised, a delicate blend of flavors on his tongue. But the taste that lingers is the vague saltiness of soy sauce on Mac's fingers before he pulls them back.

Neither Mac nor Sasha seems to notice anything wrong with what just happened, but David spends the rest of the meal lecturing himself all the same. Whatever relationship the two of them have going, whether sexual or not, it clearly works, and has for years. And they're always happy to include him, to eat lunch with him, to invite him to their place or themselves over to his.

It's stupid of him to feel jealous when they smile or laugh together, when their shoulders brush or they take turns feeding each other bites of their food. It's stupid to wonder, to wish.

Because when it comes right down to it, even if Xander is right, even if there is something there, even if they would let David in—it's too much of a risk.

David might be the captain, but Sasha and Mac support him, balance him. Anything that fucks that up, that even might come close to fucking that up, wouldn't be worth it. Especially not this season, when they're trading third and fourth place back and forth with the Thunderbirds, when a playoff slot is so close David can practically taste it.

So he focuses on his food, eating steadily through it in his best effort to replace the calories he's burned already today, to store up energy for the game tonight. He does his best to pretend that he's not painfully aware of the way Mac and Sasha interact with each other, with him.

And when they're finished, separating back to their respective homes, he pretends he doesn't wish that they were leaving together. That instead of heading home alone, to a house that's too big and too empty without any rookies to keep an eye on this season, he wants to be leaving with them.

Better to reserve his wishes for things that might actually happen.

HALF AN HOUR into what should be his pre-game nap, David can't settle. He's lost track of how many times he's changed position, from one side to another to his stomach to his back and then starting all over again. His brain just keeps doing the endless calculations—if he falls asleep now he can get this many minutes of naptime before he needs to wake up, except now it's been another five minutes, so it will only be this many minutes of sleep.

Finally, desperate to shut up his brain, he goes to the one thing he knows will work He rolls over to dig the lube out from under the extra pillow, shoving his boxers down and getting a hand around his cock. It's already half-hard, like it knew this was coming, and it doesn't take long for him to get all the way there.

He does his best just to focus on the physical sensation, the slick stroke of his hand, the lube warming under his touch. But his brain once again betrays him, slipping into fantasy before he even realizes it's happening.

"Hey, Cap," Mac says with a wicked smile as David stepped into the showers, his hand moving lazily over his cock. "Gonna wash my back?"

"Is that what you want?" David asks, something making him bold enough to move into Mac's space.

Mac's eyes drop to his mouth as David licks his lips. "Well, if you're offering..."

It's worth the ache to see Mac's eyes go wide as David sinks to his knees on the tile floor. "I'm offering," David says firmly, leaning in to close his mouth over Mac's cock.

"Jesus fuck," Mac hisses, his hands coming down to thread through David's hair. "Should've known you wouldn't fuck around, huh?"

"Da," Sasha rumbles from the door into the showers.

David tries to jerk away, but Mac isn't having any of it, hands holding him in place. "Gonna watch, Sash?" he asks, smirking down as David's cheeks go red.

"I think yes," Sasha says, moving into David's line of sight, his eyes hot and intent on them. "Not let me interrupt."

It takes a second to collect himself, but David gets

back to the matter at hand, sliding his hands up Mac's thighs just to feel the muscle flexing before moving slowly back down Mac's cock until he can't take any more.

"Fuck," Mac says again, his legs shaking under David's touch. "You're good at that."

"Look good, too," Sasha says, his voice low and rough. When David looks over, Sasha's eyes are fixed on where Mac's cock slides in and out on David's mouth. Sasha's cock is so hard it looks like it hurts, bouncing slightly as he moves behind Mac and it disappears from view. "Both look good."

Mac's breath hisses out between his teeth as David takes him deeper. "I'm—fuck, not gonna last. Don't tease me, David."

David redoubles his efforts, pulling out every trick he knows. Within a gratifyingly short amount of time, Mac's words have turned into a stream of helpless sounds, his head tipped back onto Sasha's shoulder as he comes.

Swallowing, David sits back on his heels, running his tongue over his lips to catch the last stray traces of Mac's flavor lingering there. He reaches for his own cock, so hard it won't take much to get him off.

"No," Sasha says, kissing Mac lightly before letting

go and moving around him to where David kneels on the floor. "My turn."

David turns to face him, reaching for his cock, but Sasha pulls him to his feet, leaning down to lick the taste of Mac out of his mouth. The kiss is long and lingering, leaving David breathless by the time Sasha lifts his head.

"Taste good," Sasha says, brushing David's wet hair back from his face. "Want to fuck you. Can I?"

"Y-yes," David stammers, his cock twitching between them at the thought. "Yeah, please."

The next thing he knows, Sasha is lifting him and pressing him up against the wall. David isn't exactly a small guy, even for a CHL player, but Sasha handles him like he weighs nothing. Wrapping his legs around Sasha's waist, David breathes deeply as one thick finger presses slowly inside him.

"How does he feel, babe?" Mac asks, leaning in to press a kiss to Sasha's bicep.

"Good," Sasha says, thrusting that finger in and out. "Tight."

David lets his head fall back against the wall, does his best to relax. "Another one," he breathes, rolling his hips to meet Sasha's thrusts. "I'm ready, Sash, come on."

"Not want to hurt you," Sasha says, but he starts

slowly working another finger inside. It's a stretch, but it feels amazing, to be so full, to be pinned between Sasha and the wall, Mac's hand stroking idly up and down his arm.

"I'm good, I swear." David is very close to just begging, his cock aching where it lies against his belly. "Fuck me already."

Sasha chuckles. "Bossy. Guess that's why you captain." He fucks his fingers in and out for another few strokes, until David practically writhes on them, then pulls them out and lines up his cock.

"You're gonna love this," Mac murmurs in David's ear, hand sliding down to tweak a nipple. "Sash's gonna make you feel so good—"

David lies in his bed, breathing like he just skated a twenty-minute shift. He's vaguely aware that he should feel guilty, that he will feel guilty soon enough for jerking off to fantasies of his alternate captains, his best friends.

But for now he's going to enjoy the blissful sense of quiet in his head, of peace. He's going to lie in the warm afternoon sun, let his heart rate and his breathing slow, and then he's going to get some rest.

He's asleep before he can spend too much time berating himself.

2

BO

Bo wakes up sweating, again. Which shouldn't be a surprise, because his giant Russian boyfriend likes to turn the heat up— "Can afford it! Millionaire hockey player!" Sasha always says. And then, no matter how high the thermostat is set, he always wakes up with Sasha wrapped around him like a six-foot-four octopus, their shared body heat raising a ridiculous amount of sweat.

The point is, it's gross, and the only thing that makes it worthwhile—okay, not the only thing, but a big one, in more way than one—is the fact that Bo can just roll over, pressing his lips to the sensitive spot under Sasha's jaw. He never gets tired of this, the rasp of stubble under his mouth, the taste of salt on Sasha's skin, the feeling of Sasha waking up under his hands.

"*Kotyenok*," Sasha rumbles, his eyes still closed.

Bo can't let that pass without a light pinch on the ribs. "I'm not your kitten, Aleksandr."

Sasha's big hands slide down his back, pressing their bodies together. "No? You purr for me."

"I do not," Bo sputters, resisting the urge to arch into Sasha's touch. He has a point to make here.

"Do too," Sasha says lazily, leaning down to kiss him.

Sure, Bo could continue the argument. That's fun, sometimes, arguing and play-wrestling their way through sex. But this? This is his favorite thing about being with Sasha. Making out, skin to skin, as their kisses slowly go from soft and lazy to wet and hungry.

He's not sure which of them moves—hell, maybe it's both of them, but there's a shift, and then the hot slide of Sasha's cock next to his. Bo breaks the kiss to gasp for air, not sure if he's trying to get closer or further away. "Lube," he pants, trying to remember where they left it last night.

"Here." Sasha rolls them until he's on top, reaching for the bedside table. The automatic dispenser whirs—best investment ever, Bo thinks for the trillionth time—and then Sasha leans back to get his hand between them.

"Cold!" Bo hisses at the first touch of the lube. It's probably not actually that cold, but in comparison to their body heat, it feels like ice on his cock.

Sasha nuzzles into the side of his neck, distracting him while the lube warms. "Baby," he chides, his tone fondly mocking.

"Yeah, yeah, see how you like it when it's your cock," Bo shoots back, breathless from the cold.

"Not have to," Sasha says smugly. "I warm on you first."

Bo would like to say that he's willing to not put out on principle over something like that—actually, no, fuck principle, he'd rather get laid. But either way, whatever he might have said gets lost anyway when Sasha nudges their cocks together, wrapping them in one big, capable hand.

"Fuck," he breathes, the word feeling almost like it's punched out of him.

"That's idea," Sasha snarks, but his voice is strained, like he's almost as close as Bo.

They get lost after that, no more words as they move together, fucking into the circle of Sasha's hand. Which is not to say that they're quiet—Bo has always been noisy during sex. It had taken him a few months back when they first got together to convince Sasha he really did want to hear the gasps and groans, but at this point Sasha's probably actually louder than he is.

"Close," Bo pants, his fingers digging into Sasha's biceps as he rolls his hips, chasing the sensation. "Come on,"

Sasha groans, twisting his hand on the upstroke. It's almost clumsy, but it's enough to push Bo over the edge, coming slick and hot all over Sasha's hand and his own stomach. It only takes a few more strokes before Sasha joins him, shuddering and going still for a long, frozen moment.

Eventually, though, he collapses—thankfully to the side and not directly on top of Bo, There are definitely contexts where being pinned under Sasha's two-hundred-plus pounds of muscle is hot, but right now it would just be in the temperature sense.

They lie there, both breathing like they've just been bag skated, until Sasha raises his clean hand and Bo half-heartedly slaps it.

"Good game," Sasha says solemnly.

Bo rolls his head to the side, because it's not worth lifting it, but a glare is the only appropriate response here.

Sasha is, of course, completely unfazed. "What? Teamwork. Is good."

"Not everything's a game, Sashenka," Bo mutters, not realizing he'd used the diminutive until Sasha smiles at him, soft and dopey.

"We work together." Sasha shrugs, reaching over to brush Bo's hair out of his eyes where it's flopping down over his forehead. "We achieve goal. Teamwork. Good game."

Bo rolls his eyes. "Fine. Good game. Time to hit the showers."

Sasha bounds out of bed with more energy than any one human should have at this time of the morning. "Yes! I scrub your back. Teamwork."

Allowing himself to be pulled to his feet, Bo follows his boyfriend into the bathroom. He can't even really be annoyed, honestly. He got an awesome orgasm, and now Sasha's hands are all over him, washing him off, massaging shampoo and then conditioner into his hair. They're gonna eat an awesome breakfast and then they're going to go get paid to skate around on the ice.

"Our lives are awesome," he tells Sasha, who grins at him, nudging him back under the spray.

"See?" Sasha says after a moment, his fingers combing through Bo's hair. "Purring. *Kotenyok.*"

Bo wants to deny or retaliate, but that would mean moving away from Sasha's scalp massage, and some things just aren't worth it. "Whatever," he sighs.

Sasha kisses him, softly. "*Da*," he says when he lifts his head. "Awesome."

THE REST of their morning moves with the precision of routine, smooth and practiced. Bo makes the coffee while Sasha cooks, omelets stuffed with meat and cheese and vegetables, bacon sizzling in another pan alongside.

"Real bacon?" Bo asks when the smell hits his nose, leaning against the counter by the coffee machine.

"Your weight going down," Sasha says, tilting the omelet pan to get the egg mixture fully cooked. "Need fat. Carol said."

Bo stretches, mostly for the warm feeling when

Sasha turns to watch him, and retrieves their mugs from the dishwasher. "Awww, babe, are you and Carol ganging up on me?"

Sasha hums, his verbal equivalent of a shrug. "Need to take care of yourself. Not teenager anymore."

"You take that back!" Bo distributes the coffee between their mugs, adding the sweetener and creamer Sasha likes and taking it to him with a kiss to his shoulder before settling in to watch the final stages of breakfast. "I am young at heart."

The snort he gets in reply is even more expressive than the hum, even without the look Sasha shoots him. "You mean child. You are child."

"I did warn you," Bo points out, sipping his black coffee. "I said, when we started dating—"

"I remember," Sasha says absently, sliding the omelets onto waiting plates and adding the toast waiting in the toaster. "Get butter?"

Bo pushes away from the counter reluctantly; even after, shit, almost three years together, he still likes watching Sasha cook, being in his space. But he also likes eating, and they are on something of a schedule this morning.

They demolish their food mostly in focused

silence, as usual, Bo's foot hooked around Sasha's ankle under the table. Then, as much as Bo would like to stretch out on the couch and digest, it's time to grab their bags and head to the arena for another fabulous day with the Wendigos.

They pull into arena parking behind Xander's big fuck-off pickup truck, with Xander and Jordan getting out at the same time Bo and Sasha do.

"Morning, lovebirds," Bo sing-songs as they all head into the arena.

Xander flips him off with the hand that isn't holding Jordan's—a neat trick considering that's also the hand that's wrapped around his coffee cup. "Fuck off, Mac."

"Aww, so cranky," Bo coos. "What's the matter? Did you have to sleep on the couch? Piss your boy off already?"

The corner of Jordan's mouth twitches up, but he doesn't say anything, and neither does Xander, settling for a deeply unamused look.

"Leave Richie alone," Sasha rumbles, his hand landing on the back of Bo's neck.

"Thanks," Xander says, hitching his bag up a little higher on his shoulder.

Sasha nods solemnly in answer. "Richie not bird. Big, annoying puppy dog."

"Hey!" Xander's indignant expression melts into something softer when Jordan laughs. It's kind of disgustingly cute, but Bo decides he's reached his allotted amount of relationship chirps for the day. He'll just have to save that for the next time Xander snows him in practice.

Jordan peels off once they reach the trainers room, with Xander lingering for a goodbye kiss that skirts right up to the line of being inappropriate for the workplace. Bo shakes his head as he and Sasha continue toward the locker room, dropping their gear off before heading to the gym for a warm-up.

"You're late," David says from the assault bike as they come in the door, hardly out of breath even though his shirt is damp with the sweat glistening on his face. It's a good look, or it would be if not for the pinched scowl on his face.

Bo checks the clock and exchanges a look with Sasha. "Uh, it's just now eleven?"

"Early is on time, on time is late," David says tersely, picking up the pace before they can respond.

Sasha shakes his head minutely, so Bo bites back his retort and starts on his own warm-up. Maybe by the time David gets off the bike he'll be over whatever crawled up his ass and ready to calm down.

Unfortunately, that doesn't seem to be the case.

He's snappy on the ice too, until Ads and Rosie look like they're about to cry. Sasha has to take them aside for a little alternate captain damage control—and some extra defense drills, since they really could use the work.

That seems to get through to David—a good thing, too, because Bo wasn't looking forward to being the A visibly yelling at their captain during practice like he'd been gearing up to do. David manages to be polite for the rest of practice, but the vertical line between his eyebrows and the tightness of his jaw are still there when everyone filters back into the locker room.

Unfortunately, Bo can tell just from the set of his shoulders, the way he's holding himself apart from everyone else, that talking to him isn't going to do any good right now. They'll have to give him a little time.

So he showers off, begs some hot tub time off of Jordan—Niki's slap-shot hit him hard enough to bruise even through the pads and Sasha's right, he isn't as young as he used to be—and holds his tongue

Until they're in the car and heading home.

"What the fuck is David's problem?" he asks as soon as the doors are closed.

Sasha shrugs. "Worried about playoffs."

Which, yeah, but— "We're all worried about the playoffs," Bo points out, backing out of their parking space and heading for the street. It's dumb, to act like talking about the possibility of the playoffs is going to keep the Wendigos from making it, but fuck, Bo's been playing hockey since he was three, he can't help it if he's superstitious.

"David worry more," Sasha points out, which, yes, also true. "Also, maybe needs get laid?"

As much as Bo loves that Sasha feels comfortable enough not to worry too much about his English when it's just the two of them, it takes him awhile to parse that sentence. "That—okay, yeah. It's been awhile since he dated anyone. You're probably right."

Sasha nods. "Dating hard, with hockey. Take time."

"Yeah." As usual, there's no way Bo can argue with that. "Hey, maybe we could get him a fleshlight or something? Just until the—until the season's over?"

He honestly says it like, seventy-five percent for Sasha's unamused look. His boyfriend does not disappoint. Bo grins back, chuckling all the way home.

Halfway through his salmon and broccoli at dinner, Bo drops his fork with a clatter. When Sasha doesn't look up from his own plate, he follows it up with an ostentatious throat clearing.

"Bone stuck in throat?" Sasha asks, cutting off a piece of his chicken breast.

"No. I just had the best idea."

That gets him a look, Sasha's eyes narrowed as he chews and swallows. "Okay," he finally says, his voice far more resigned than it should be for someone who claims to love Bo.

"Okay, hear me out. David needs somebody, but who has time to fucking date at this point in the season?"

Sasha shrugs. "Could fuck teammate. Is what I do."

"I'm ignoring that, because we both know you love me," Bo says cheerfully. "Getting back to my point, you know David's not going to start hitting on some random guy from the team. He takes that captain shit seriously. So we're going to help him out."

"Like matchmaker?" Sasha asks, his expression, if possible, becoming even more skeptical.

It's Bo's turn to shrug. "Maybe. But in the meantime, we'll be his temporary boyfriends. Have him over for dinner more often, cuddles, that kind of thing. Keep him from getting so lonely and wound so tight."

Sasha purses his lips, his face scrunching into his adorable thinking expression. "Does temporary boyfriend mean sex?"

"Can you imagine David going for that?" Bo laughs, picking up his fork.

"Yeah," Sasha says, his voice gone low and rough in a way that makes Bo freeze, a forkful of salmon halfway to his mouth.

He forces his hand to start moving again. "Goddamnit, Sash. No. The last time this happened the food was cold and disgusting after. Finish your dinner before you start talking dirty to me."

Sasha grins back at him. "I have good imagination."

"Fuck you, I know. Eat your damn dinner."

They plow through the food in record time even for them; Bo is vaguely surprised that neither of them choke, honestly. Sasha keeps quiet until they're loading their dishes into the dishwasher, crowding Bo up against the counter as soon as he closes the door. "Now?"

Bo shivers a little when Sasha's fingers slip under his t-shirt. "Fine, yes, now."

"Would look so good," Sasha breathes, pushing Bo's shirt up and over his head. "You and David. Think he fuck you like you like?"

"Fuck," Bo groans, getting his hands on Sasha's ass and pulling him in closer. "You'd like that?"

Sasha nods, leaning down for a deep, filthy kiss before lifting his head, lips curved in the little smirk that shouldn't be so attractive. "Maybe I fuck him while he fucks you, hmm? Would be hot."

"Keep talking like that and this is going to be over really fast," Bo warns.

He sucks in a sharp breath when Sasha shoves his sweats down, letting them fall to the floor, then picks him up and set him on the counter. "What—?"

Sasha winks as he wraps a hand around Bo's cock and starts to stroke. "Like that?"

"Fuck, yeah," Bo breathes. "So you'd want—you'd be okay with David? Me with David?"

"Would be hot," Sasha repeats. "Open him up while he fucks you."

Bo shudders, the words and the sensations working together to have him embarrassingly close to the edge. "God, yeah. Watching you fuck him—shit, Sash, I'm so close."

"Come," Sasha rumbles, twisting his hand around the head on the upstroke. "Come for me, *kotyenok*."

"Fuck," Bo gasps, his body arching up into Sasha's grip as he comes.

When he blinks his eyes open after, he realizes he came all over Sasha's t-shirt. "Shit," he laughs, his voice a little hoarse. "That's gonna be a bitch to clean."

Sasha just shrugs, peeling out of the shirt and dropping it in the sink. "Is fine. A little soap, cold water, like new. Besides. Worth it."

Bo drags him in closer, getting a hand down his pants to find his cock, hard and slick, the foreskin drawn back below the head. "What do you want, huh, babe? Want my mouth? Or I could jerk you off while I talk about us fucking David."

"*Blyad*," Sasha mutters, his eyes fluttering closed. "Talk, *detka*."

"You're right," Bo breathes, stroking a little slower than he knows Sasha likes, just to tease. "It would be hot. I bet I could feel it, the way he'd move while you opened him up. Feel his cock twitching inside me. Do you think he'd be quiet, when you're balls-deep inside him? I bet we could get him to make noise, when you're fucking both of us."

Sasha groans, thrusting up into Bo's grip. "*Da, jebat.*"

"Gonna feel so fucking good," Bo says, running his free hand up to tease at one of Sasha's nipples. "Or maybe we let him fuck my mouth while you fuck my ass, fill me up—"

He cuts off his litany when Sasha comes hot and slick all over his hand. He slumps against the counter, his head dropping to rest on Bo's shoulder.

They stay like that for a few minutes, just breathing, before Sasha steps back, giving Bo room to slip down from the counter and wash his hands in the side of the sink that doesn't contain a semen-stained t-shirt.

"Well, that was—slightly unexpected," he says over his shoulder. "You're going to wipe down the counter, right?"

He looks over to see Sasha doing just that, biting his lip like he's worried about something. "What?"

"Was okay?" Sasha mumbles, not looking up. "Not cross line?"

"Hey, no." Bo dries his hands hastily, closing

the space between them and wrapping his arms around Sasha's waist. "It was great. Seriously, super hot, no lines crossed. C'mon, let's go cuddle on the couch and watch dumb people make bad choices."

Sasha meets his eyes then, searching for reassurance, before kissing him lightly and pushing him in the direction of the living room. "Be there in minute. Shirt needs to soak."

"Fine," Bo sighs, retrieving his sweats and pulling them back on, leaving his boxers on the floor. "But I'm not restarting the episode for you, so work fast."

True to his word, Sasha joins him on the couch before Hulu has completely finished loading. Bo starts an episode of *Real Housewives of Orange County* and tosses the remote onto the coffee table before snuggling into Sasha's side.

"He probably wouldn't actually go for sex," he says with a sigh after about ten minutes of rich people acting baffled when their entitled kids make stupid choices.

Bo can feel Sasha nodding his agreement. "Probably."

"That's okay, though," Bo says, doing his best to ignore the fact that they both sound a little wistful.

"He can get laid anywhere. We're here for the other stuff. Right?"

"Right."

Bo turns his attention back to the TV and doesn't spend even a little bit of energy wishing David would be interested in sex with them.

3

SASHA

"If you think—" David's rant cuts off when Sasha slides in between him and Dino, blocking his line of sight. "Sasha, what—"

"Have minute?"

Sasha phrases it as a question, but he moves into David's space as he does so. Not fast and aggressive, because that will just get David pushing back, but slowly. Behind him, he hears Dino taking advantage of the distraction to rejoin the rest of the team for shooting drills.

"I—" David presses his lips together, a muscle flexing in his jaw, then blows out a breath. "Sure, Sash. What's up?"

"Was thinking defense need add skating drills," Sasha says the first thing that comes to his mind.

"Speed, uh, what's word, *podvizhnost*, uh, shit. Agility?"

David's expression clears, but he still looks a little pinched around the edges, his shoulders so tense it's visible even under his pads and practice jersey. "That's not a bad idea, but our practices are already pretty long. We don't want to wear them out, not this early in the season."

"Yeah." Sasha considers, because he might have just blurted it out, but it's not a bad idea. Their defense isn't slow, exactly, but speed and agility would definitely help. "Maybe for warm-up?"

"That might work," David says, giving him a tight smile. "I'll talk to Coach after we're done today."

Before he can leave and find some other hapless teammate to berate, Sasha skates closer, bumps his arm gently into David's shoulder. "Dinner tonight? Making blini and shashlyk."

"I shouldn't..." David hesitates, visibly torn.

Sasha rolls his eyes and manages to refrain from commenting. "Chicken shashlyk. And broccoli. Meal plan is okay."

"Okay," David says finally. "Seven?"

"Da." Sasha claps him on the shoulder and turns to skate away before David can change his mind. Maybe it's his imagination, but it seems like David is just slightly less on edge for the rest of the practice. Possibly. It's hard to be sure.

When practice is finally over and the team troops back into the locker room, Sasha pauses by Bo's stall. "You right," he says quietly, pitching his voice below the good-natured chirping that fills the room.

"I'm always right," Bo shoots back, just as quiet while he's taking off his blockers. "What am I right about this time?"

Sasha snorts. "David. Dinner tonight."

"Check." Bo says. "Go shower, you stink."

"Is manly stink," Sasha says louder, giving Bo a facewash with his sweaty glove.

Bo tries to move away, but with Sasha blocking his exit, there's nowhere for him to go. "Ugh, Cap, help!"

"Nobody can help you, Mac," David calls from across the room. "You're on your own."

"Awww, I thought you loved me," Bo pouts, shrinking back into his stall as far as he can go.

David just shakes his head, bending over to unlace his skates.

Sasha grins down at Bo, lingering just long enough to prove his point before making his way to his own stall, finally. As he starts to strip out of his sweaty gear, part of his mind is busy making a grocery list, while the rest is still poking at the David problem.

He'd been a little skeptical when Bo first brought it up, but David really is wound too tight for this early in the season. He's still not entirely sure Bo's plan is going to work, but it's worth a try. If it gets David to stop riding the team so hard, good. And it's not like it's that much different from the way the three of them usually hang out.

He steadfastly ignores the little voice telling him that they've never hung out after he and Bo got off to the idea of fucking David. As much as he hates to admit it, he can't think of a better way to help calm David down. Not without actually fucking him, anyway, and as tightly wound as he is right now, there's no telling what the fallout would be if they suggest it.

The team doesn't need their captain snapping at everyone, but they sure as hell need him to be working with his A's, not avoiding them because of an unfortunate proposition. So Sasha will make shashlyk and blinis and Bo will coax David into cuddling and everything will be fine.

Three hockey players cuddling on a couch, because

two of them are definitely gay, Sasha thinks with a snort and goes to take his shower.

SASHA IS TOSSING broccoli florets with olive oil when the doorbell rings.

"I told him," Bo sighs, heading for the door. "He has a key. He could come in."

"Is polite," Sasha says absently, spreading the broccoli evenly across the parchment paper and sliding it into the hot oven. "David is nice boy."

"Hopefully not that nice!" Bo throws back over his shoulder just as he opens the door. "Oh Captain, my Captain!"

David's snort is audible in the kitchen, but he steps inside as Sasha turns to look. "You know, that was old like, the second time you did it, right?"

"Can't stop, won't stop," Bo retorts, pulling David in for a bro-hug. "C'mon, Sash's almost done with dinner. I'm helping by not touching anything."

"Solid plan," David says dryly, setting a six-pack of bottles on the counter as he follows Bo into the kitchen. "I brought beer."

Sasha nods. "Good. Have beer, relax. I grill shashlik and we eat."

"Sure I can't do anything?" David asks, grabbing the bottle opener off the fridge and cracking open three bottles.

"Is done." Sasha accepts his beer and pulls David in for a hug of his own, possibly lingering a little longer that is strictly bro-level.

David doesn't pull away until he lets go, though. And even then, he doesn't go far, leaning back against the counter next to the stove and taking a drink of his beer, his cheeks a little more flushed under the usual warm brown of his skin than the heat from the stove can account for.

Bo moans almost pornographically when he drinks as well. "Holy shit, Cap, where did you find this beer? This is some good shit."

David shrugs. "The guy at the liquor store recommended it when I asked for a good stout."

"Awww, you remembered," Bo coos, fluttering his eyelashes at David as he takes another drink. "My hero."

Sasha rolls his eyes, lifting the skewers of chicken out of the marinade and placing them carefully on the grill plate. "What I, chopped liver?"

"I dunno, babe," Bo says, sidling in to wrap an arm around his waist. "You don't buy me beer. Maybe you need to step up your game."

He laughs at the rude noise Sasha makes in return. "You take, Cap," Sasha says, watching David out of the corner of his eye for a reaction, his stomach in knots despite knowing he has nothing to fear here. "He hog blankets, kick all night."

"No thanks," David says, his wide eyes the only indication of surprise. It's an impressive poker face. "I'm not about to get in the middle of you two."

Bo very nearly chokes on the sip of beer he'd just taken and Sasha can feel his own cheeks heating as he turns the skewers on the grill.

David looks back and forth between them, clearly trying to figure out their reaction, but in the end all he says is, "So you two are actually together, huh?"

"Yeah," Sasha agrees, since Bo is still wheezing slightly. "Problem?"

"No," David says, meeting his eyes squarely. "You've clearly been making it work for…however long it's been going on…without affecting the team. As long as it stays that way, it's none of my business. But—why keep it a secret?"

Bo shrugs. "At first, we didn't want people to feel like they had to take sides if it ended badly, you know? And by the time we figured out we were solid, it was just habit. I'm a very private person, you know."

Sasha and David both snort at that, making eye contact automatically. Sasha can't help grinning, and David grins back.

"Yeah, everybody knows that about you," David says, rolling his eyes at Sasha.

Any further comment is cut off when the oven timer beeps, obnoxiously loud as always. Sasha slips his hand into an oven mitt and pulls out the roasted broccoli, beautifully caramelized and sizzling. The chicken is almost done when he checks it, but there's the slightest bit of pink when he cuts into one of the larger pieces, so he turns them again. "Get plates?" he asks.

"I can do it," David says, even though the question had been directed at Bo.

Their kitchen is large, part of the reason Sasha had picked this apartment in the first place, but none of them are exactly small. Still, they're used to close quarters. There's no real reason Sasha should be feeling like a teenager with his first crush over David's proximity, the way he brushes up against Bo as he sets three plates on the counter and opens the silverware drawer.

"Is ready," Sasha announces finally, distributing

the skewers between their plates, then the broccoli. "Go, sit. Eat."

David takes his plate and leads the way to their dining table, Bo and Sasha following behind him.

"Looks great, babe," Bo says, picking up a skewer. "But I thought I was promised blinis?"

"Eat dinner first," Sasha says, rolling his eyes. "Then blinis."

David takes a bite of his own chicken. "Yeah, Mac, eat your vegetables first."

"Ugh, no fair teaming up on me," Bo pouts.

Sasha is incredibly grateful his mouth is empty so he doesn't choke like Bo did earlier. "Maybe act like adult, then," is all he says, taking a sip of his beer and trying desperately to get his mind out of the gutter. Although that was probably Bo's intention, considering the little smirk on his face.

Thankfully, David takes the opportunity to change the subject. They spend the rest of dinner discussing skating drills for the d-men, how much ham and turkey is too much to order for half of a CHL team's Thanksgiving dinner, and ways to improve the efficiency of their line changes. Before Sasha knows it, Bo and David are giving him identical puppy-dog eyes over their empty plates.

"Fine," he sighs, heaving himself up from his

chair maybe a bit more dramatically than necessary. "Blinis. Get jam."

The oven is still hot, so he retrieves the foil-wrapped packages from the freezer and slides them directly onto the rack. Ten minutes later, he stacks the reheated blinis onto a plate and carries them to the table, sneaking the top two onto his own plate before letting Bo and David attack the rest.

"Ugh," David groans, sitting back from the table. "I should not have had that last one."

"It's fine," Bo says airily. "You'll skate it off tomorrow. Carb-loading the night before a game is just good sense. C'mon, let's go watch a movie while we digest."

David pushes to his feet and reaches for his plate, but Bo pulls it away before he can grab it. "Nah, I've got the dishes. You go with Sash, make sure he doesn't pick something depressing and Russian."

"Hey," Sasha says mildly. "Was one time."

"Sure, babe." Bo pats him gently on the arm. "Keep telling yourself that. I'm begging you, Cap. Something with explosions. Help me, Obi-Wan. You're my only hope."

David rolls his eyes, but he's smiling when he

joins Sasha on the couch. "How have you not stran-gled him by now?"

Sasha shrugs as he picks up the remote. "Is good in bed. Very good."

It's worth it for the way David sputters, barely managing not to spray his beer all over the couch. "Jesus, Sasha."

"What? Is true." Sasha shrugs again. "Good with hands."

"Not to toot my own horn, but yeah." Bo circles around the couch. "Scoot over, Cap."

David does so automatically, then frowns. "Don't you want to—"

"Nope," Bo says, plopping down in the empty space, half on top of David. "I get to sit next to him all the time. This is captain and alternate captain cuddle time."

"I, uh—"

Bo throws his legs over David's lap, his heels landing on Sasha's thigh. "Nope. No escape."

"Fine," David grumbles, settling back against the cushions, his shoulder bumping Sasha's arm. "I guess I'm stuck."

"Yup." Bo pokes Sasha with his toes. "C'mon, babe. Movie time."

Sasha grins. "Anna Karenina, *da?*"

"Nooooo," Bo groans, drumming his heels on Sasha's thigh like a toddler having a tantrum. "Back me up here, Cap. Explosions and guns and lots of thinly-veiled homoerotic subtext."

"I dunno," David says with a smirk. "Jude Law was pretty hot in that."

Sasha nods, lifting the remote. "*Da*, is what I'm saying!"

"No!" Bo launches himself over David to try and wrestle the remote away from Sasha. "Never!"

It's not exactly much of a contest, considering how much taller Sasha is than Bo, but after a few minutes of token struggle, Sasha hands over the remote, stealing a kiss in the process. "Fine. You pick."

"Oh, I will," Bo crows, settling back halfway on David's lap and hooking an arm around his neck as he navigates to some mindless summer blockbuster. "Sit back and enjoy, boys."

Sasha keeps waiting for David to protest, but he just wraps an arm around Bo's waist, his expression caught halfway between exasperation and fondness as he looks at the screen.

4

DAVID

David is losing his mind.

He's used to Sasha and Bo being around. They're on the same team. For the length of the hockey season, the Wendigos spend eight or more hours a day in each other's company. And that doesn't even take into account the way David needs to work with his A's. He spends more time with Sasha and Bo than some people spend with their spouses.

But now it seems like they're always around. Or maybe it's a heightened awareness now that he knows for sure that they're together. Either way, they feel inescapable. On the ice, in the locker room, on the plane. At meals.

And they're always touching him. Nothing out

of the ordinary for a hockey team, really. Nothing that anyone else would notice or comment on. But somehow every brush of Sasha's fingers over the back of his neck, every time Bo slings an arm around his shoulders, every look he catches from either of them, feels loaded with secret significance.

He can't remember jerking off this much in his life.

He makes an effort to be the last one in the showers, circling the locker room to talk to Xander about his shoulder, see how Harty's knee is holding up. But somehow, no matter how long he lingers, either Bo or Sasha—or both—is always in the showers when he makes his way in.

He almost never has the kind of privacy for even a quick, furtive jerk, always has to mentally tally up the number of wins they need to clinch a playoff spot in order to keep his idiot cock under control.

He makes it through the next few days on sheer willpower, sneaking into bathrooms for a few minutes alone when he can't deal with the tension anymore. The only time he feels safe enough to really let himself go is at night, when he's alone in his bed. He's given up on pretending that he's not going to do this.

Honestly, who does it hurt? Not Bo and Sasha, stupidly happy together and probably fucking each other at this very moment. If it hurts anyone, it's David, but he can't help but get wrapped up in the mental picture, the fantasy. Imagining what might have happened if their dinner and a movie the other night had gone just a bit differently...

David shivers as Bo's fingers play up and down the side of his neck, sparks of sensation dancing across his skin.

"Cold?" Bo murmurs, shifting position on his lap like he can't feel David's cock, half-hard under his ass.

"No." David glances over at Sasha, waiting for his nod before slipping his hand under the hem of Bo's t-shirt, fingertips sliding slowly, teasingly across skin, nudging just under the waistband of his sweats. "You?"

Bo arches his back, shamelessly pushing up into David's touch. "Not cold. But if somebody doesn't get a hand on my cock soon, I'm gonna have to do it myself."

"That might be hot," David muses, smiling at the annoyed huff he gets in response. But as hot as he's sure it would be, sitting here with Sasha, watching Bo jerk

himself off for them, that's not going to satisfy his need for touch, for skin.

Kissing Bo's neck is easy, it's right there, and it distracts him just long enough for David to get a hand down his pants. "No underwear?" he breathes, watching goosebumps rise on the skin that's still wet from his mouth as he wraps a hand around Bo's cock and gives it one long, slow stroke. "Someone was hopeful."

"Figured you or Sash'd take 'em off me," Bo gasps, thrusting into his hand when it doesn't move further. "C'mon, please."

"What do you think?" David asks, meeting Sasha's eyes, hot and intent as he watches them, one hand pressing down against the bulge in his own sweats.

Sasha hums, pushing his sweats down enough that his cock springs free, hard and flushed, the foreskin pulled back below the head. "Da, touch him. Show me."

Bo whines his protest when David lets go of his cock, but obediently lifts his hips enough for David to push the sweats down to his knees, kicks them impatiently to the floor.

"Shirt too," Sasha orders, his hand moving slowly over his cock. "Want him naked for us."

David curls his hands in the hem of Bo's shirt,

pulling it up and over his head. He has no idea where it ends up after that and he doesn't care.

The word "us" still echoes in his ears, the intimacy of it. The solemn note in Sasha's voice, like he was trusting David with something infinitely precious, the way Bo's body curves into David's as he settles back—they're overwhelming. So David does what he does best and narrows his focus.

"Fuck, yes," Bo breathes, head falling back onto David's shoulder when his hand wraps around his cock again. "Just like that. Always—fuck—knew you had good hands."

"If you make a stick-handling joke right now you have to finish this yourself," David threatens, but he keeps his hand moving, slides his free hand up to brush a thumb over Bo's nipple.

Bo grinds his ass down against David's cock, alternately moving away from and toward David's touch. "Oh fuck. I'm so close."

"Look good," Sasha rumbles. When David glances over, the intensity of Sasha's gaze seems to sear through him. "Make him come. Want to see."

"Hear that?" David murmurs into Bo's ear, holding Sasha's eyes with his own. "I'm gonna make you come all over yourself while we watch."

"*Fuck,*" *Bo whimpers, his whole body shaking, his breath catching in his throat. "Fuck, fuck, fuck—*"

He arches up off of David's lap as he comes, hot spurts coating his stomach and David's fist. Sasha watches intently, his hand moving faster on his cock, until Bo settles back against David with a sigh.

David loosens his grip on Bo's cock slowly, soothing the shivers racing through his body with his other hand, firm on his stomach. He's just wondering what to do with his messy hand, reluctant to disturb Bo, when Sasha reaches for it, bringing it to his mouth.

Sasha cleans his hand with long, slow strokes of his tongue, sucking each finger slowly into his mouth, scraping his teeth gently over David's thumb. David didn't think it was possible for him to get any harder, but his cock happily proves him wrong.

"What you want?" Sasha asks quietly.

"I, uh..." David's mind briefly shuts down, unable to parse the possible options, to consider them logically. "I want to see you and Bo. Together."

Sasha smiles, slow and happy. "Is okay, kotyenok?"

Bo stretches langorously on David's lap, the press of his ass a torturous tease against David's cock, then slides into Sasha's lap, straddling his massive thighs. "Yeah, we can do that. How do you want me, babe?"

"Hmmm." Sasha pulls him in for a kiss, deep and wet and filthy. "On knees."

It only takes a few seconds of watching them together, Bo on his knees while Sasha thrusts carefully into his mouth, hands fisted in his hair, before David has to shove his sweats down and get a hand on his cock. He comes almost embarrassingly quickly, but Sasha follows soon after, pulling out to come all over Bo's chest.

David lies in his bed and waits for his heart rate to come back down, his breathing to return to normal. Eventually, though, he forces himself to get up, to clean off in the bathroom. He'll have to live with the fact that he jerked off to his friends and teammates—again—in the morning, but at least he won't be scraping dried jizz out of his happy trail while he does so.

And at least the roadie that starts tomorrow will give him something else to think about besides this stupid, childish crush, he thinks as he finally drifts off to sleep.

HE KNOWS PERFECTLY WELL that he's deluding himself, but he doesn't expect the delusion to be stripped away so quickly. But as soon as he settles in on the plane, Mac drops into the seat next to him, chattering away about something, and Sasha settles in across the little table, smiling indulgently at both of them.

And sure, this is how they normally sit for roadies, touching base about a million and one little team things. It's probably his own fault, that now everything feels loaded with significance. He's over-analyzing the way Mac is always leaning in so their arms press together on the armrest, the way he sits with his legs spread so his knee bumps against David's. And Sasha's legs are so long, surely their ankles always get tangled together.

It's not their fault. It's not even that bad, objec-tively. He'd expected it to make him jittery and uncomfortable, about to jump out of his skin. But it's actually kind of nice. He can forget, for whole minutes at a time, that it's not real. But eventually, it always comes rushing back, leaving a hollow ache in his chest.

By the time they hit the ground in Dallas, the ache is nearly constant. As constant as Mac and Sasha, who follow him into the waiting shuttle van. Who sit with him at dinner, who find enough things that they still need to talk about after dinner that they end up following him up to his room. And he's too weak to indicate, in word or in deed, that every casual touch is slowly breaking him apart.

In the end, it's almost ten before he's alone in his room, slumping back on the bed and letting out a long breath. Perversely, after spending most of the day wishing they'd go away, now the room feels empty without them.

Lonely.

He falls asleep wondering what it would be like to have two other bodies in the big, king-sized bed.

THEY WIN 2-1 against the Thunderbirds, taking an early lead in the first that they manage to hold onto by the skin of their teeth and some really spectacular saves that leave David wondering, not for the first time, if Bo actually has magical powers. They lose to the Jackalopes in OT, in a tight shootout, but pull off a 3-2 win over the Yetis and keep the streak going with a 4-1 victory against the Werewolves before they head off to Alberta to face the Abs.

It happens almost at the end of the second period, when everyone is tired and just trying to hold out until the buzzer. It's not anyone's fault, but that doesn't change what happens.

Plata, the Abs' fourth-line forward, trips and goes sprawling. Rosie and Parks nearly collide trying to avoid him. David watches helplessly from the bench as Michaelson tries, and fails, to jump over his teammate, to keep the wickedly sharp blades of his skates away from his teammate's vulnerable body.

Everything seems to happen in slow motion as Michaelson flies through the air. David can tell even before he hits that it's going to be bad, but the sickening crack of his helmet meeting the ice stuns the arena into silence.

Worse than the sound, though, is the wrong angle of Michaelson's arm as he hits, the limp, unconscious sprawl of his body across the ice when he finally lands. Even though he's on the other team, David feels sick just watching.

All the players freeze even before the whistle—well, almost all. Petrov turns so quickly that he slides the last few feet on his knees, clearly forcing himself not to touch Michaelson's unconscious body. The medics are there almost as fast, from what David can see, although his view is obstructed by the various players on the ice, watching solemnly.

It's clear, soon enough, even with all the players standing around, that Michaelson isn't getting to his feet. There's a collective inhale and murmur from the crowd as the medics lift him onto the stretcher, strap him in and wheel him off the ice.

Luckily the officials rule the period over, adding the remaining seconds to the third period. Neither team seems able to shake off what just happened, the sudden near-finality of it all. It's a relief when the buzzer sounds and they can troop back to the visitor's locker room. Can be with their team.

David feels the heaviness as much as anyone, but he forces himself to make the rounds, to check in on his guys and get their minds back in the game. He's aware of Bo and Sasha doing the same thing, and where normally the constant awareness of their location would irritate him, now it just feels comforting. Familiar, like ice under his skates.

They continue their win streak, ending the game with a score of 2-0, but it feels like a hollow victory with the Abs so obviously shaken. It doesn't feel like a win.

As soon as they get back to the locker room,

David digs his phone out of his bag, shoots a text off to Stewart, the Abs captain. He forces himself to put it away after that—he's not going to get an immediate response, and he has responsibilities to his own team. They played a hell of a game, even with everything that happened, and it's his job to remind them of that.

Mac and Sasha have already started, he sees when he looks up. Mac is huddled with LK and Ricky, gesticulating wildly enough to have both of them smiling and laughing. Sasha has his own little cluster of d-men in the opposite corner, the conversation quieter, somehow, but David can see just as many smiles.

He's about to get up and do his part when his phone dings from inside the bag. Every head in the locker room whips around as he digs it out, conversations dying down, every player thinking about how it could so easily have been them.

The text is short and to the point, but David feels himself relaxing muscles he hadn't known were tensed. When he clears his throat, and looks up, the room goes completely silent, clearly waiting for the verdict.

"Michaelson woke up," he says, and the whole team seems to exhale as one. "Concussion for sure, broken arm, but Stewart says they're pretty sure his spine's okay. He'll be on IR for awhile, but as far as the docs know he should make a full recovery."

"Good," Sasha says, somehow materializing close enough to clap David on the shoulder. "Now we celebrate, yes?"

David knows it's weak, but he can't stop himself from leaning into the touch, just for a second. "Yeah. I'm buying drinks for everybody who got a point tonight, so get your sweaty asses into the shower!"

The noise level in the room quickly gets back to normal as most of the team returns to peeling themselves out of their gear. "Good," Sasha says again, softer but still audible under cover of the noise, squeezing David's shoulder. "You have press?"

"Ugh," David grimaces. After an injury like Michaelson's, the questions aren't going to be pleasant. "Yeah. I'm definitely gonna need a drink after that."

Sasha squeezes one more time before letting go. "I buy."

David pushes down the little voice reminding him that this isn't real. He can worry about that later. "Deal."

5

BO

"We need a Plan B," Bo announces, sneaking a slice of carrot off the cutting board. Well, trying to; Sasha clearly sees him, but just as clearly decides it's not worth commenting. It's part of why they work so well together.

"Plan B?" Sasha asks, slicing the last of the carrots before turning to check the pot of new potatoes boiling merrily away on the stove.

Bo chews and swallows before responding. "Yeah, for David. Pretend boyfriending worked at first, but ever since we got back from the roadie, he's been even worse. I thought he was gonna make Elvis cry yesterday at practice."

Sasha pokes one of the potatoes with a fork,

frowning at it for a moment before returning to the carrots. "Was rough roadie. With—" he makes a broad gesture that somehow encompasses the exhaustion of five games in a row on the road and the absolute shitstorm that had been Michaelson's injury while they were in Edmonton. "Press was bad."

"That's an understatement," Bo mutters, shuddering at the memory. He's never seen David quite so close to punching a reporter as when the dude managed to insinuate that the Wendigos had somehow set Michaelson up to nearly break his neck. "But he can't last like this. The last thing we need is our captain out with an ulcer or what the fuck ever else."

"So what's plan?" Sasha asks, tossing the carrots and the pile of broccoli on the cutting board with olive oil, adding salt and pepper from his little grinder set, and spreading them out on the parchment paper.

Bo hesitates—he'd gotten as far as needing a plan, not making one. "I don't suppose you have any brilliant ideas?"

"You make plan, I execute," Sasha says dryly, pulling the salmon out of the fridge. "I not idea guy."

"Fuck you, you have great ideas," Bo retorts, shamelessly ogling Sasha's ass as he bends over to put the vegetables in the oven. "It was your idea to hook up that first time."

Sasha shoots him a look. "Only because someone look at my ass for half season but not make move."

"Hey, it worked," Bo says with a shrug. "And it's a great ass. You can't blame me."

Sasha rolls his eyes, but leans in for a kiss before turning back to the stove. Bo watches in silence as he drops the salmon into a skillet, then turns off the burner under the potatoes and carries the pot to the sink to drain the water out.

"Maybe," Bo says slowly, "what we actually need is Plan A, continued."

When he doesn't elaborate immediately, Sasha throws a questioning look over his shoulder.

"Plan A worked for awhile, right?" He doesn't wait for an affirmative answer, because Sasha knows better than to interrupt when he's thinking out loud. "So maybe we need to step it up. The boyfriend-type stuff was good, we just didn't take it far enough."

"Sex?" Sasha says, his tone skeptical. "You think David wants?"

Bo laughs. "He looks at your ass too sometimes, babe. I know he wants. The trick is going to be getting him to go for it."

The timer beeps, and Bo maybe gets a little distracted by watching Sasha assemble their dinner onto the plates like some kind of food wizard— look, he's a simple man, and he likes being fed almost as much as his boyfriend likes feeding him. As always, the food is amazing, and he's almost forgotten what they were talking about by the time they're settled at the table and he's happily shoving salmon, roasted vegetables, and mashed potatoes into his mouth.

"You too," Sasha says between bites.

"Me too what?" he mumbles.

Sasha rolls his eyes again. It's a good thing it's so cute, because he does that a lot. "David look at your ass, too."

"See?" Bo forks up another bite of salmon. "This is gonna be easy."

Bo saunters over to David's stall, wearing nothing but one of the scratchy locker room towels wrapped around his hips—look, sacrifices have to be made sometimes. He'll make it up to his dick later.

"Good practice," he says, plopping down so close to David that all it would take is a few inches over to be sitting in his lap instead.

"Eh," David mumbles, looking anywhere but at him. "We still need to be getting more shots on goal. Did you, uh, need something?"

Bo nudges him with his shoulder. "Just making sure we're still good for Thanksgiving tomorrow. Anything else you need me or Sash to take care of?"

"No, the catering's ordered—you guys got the pies, right? There's no fucking way we can get pies this week—"

"Relax, Cap," Bo interrupts. "We ordered the pies weeks ago. And we're picking up the last of the drinks tonight. It's gonna be great."

David slumps back against his stall. "Okay. Then I guess we're good."

"Sweet." David still won't look at him, so Bo ups the ante, setting a hand on his thigh. It's warm, the muscle flexing under the thin fabric of his compression shorts. He maybe gets lost for a second before he remembers what he's supposed to be doing. "You're coming over for dinner tonight, right?"

"I, uh, I can't." David meets his eyes for a split second before looking away. "Gotta make sure everything's clean and ready for tomorrow."

Bo blinks. "Don't you have a housekeeping service?"

"Yeah, but…" David's voice trails off, a muscle jumping in his jaw as he stands. "I just can't, okay? I'll see you tomorrow."

"Okay," Bo says, frowning a little as David strips out of his shorts and heads for the shower. "Text us if you think of anything else."

David doesn't look back. "Sure."

Sasha catches Bo's eye from across the locker room, eyebrows raised. Bo shrugs and heads back to his own stall to get dressed, his brain busily working away, restructuring the plan.

It's fine. David's just trying to make everything perfect, like he always does. That's fine. Bo and Sasha will do their part, everything will be great, and they'll make their move when they're cleaning up after everyone leaves.

Everything is fine.

"Oh, God," Singer groans, slumping back in his

chair. "Who let me eat three pieces of pie? I'm gonna die."

"We tried to stop you," Bo says unsympathetically, discreetly undoing the top button of his dress slacks under the table. "But you sneaked the pecan while Sash was distracted with babies. It's your own damn fault."

Sasha nods firmly, in between cooing at Molly's six-month-old daughter. "*Da.* Right, *mishka*?"

"Hey, why does she get to be a bear?" Bo asks, pouting.

"Is fierce," Sasha says, smirking at him for a second before turning his attention to little Alina, who seems very pleased with the description, or maybe the faces he's making. "Yes? Fierce little bear. Rawr."

Bo tells himself very firmly that now is not the time to go all gooey inside over his big, beefy boyfriend trying to coax a baby into roaring like a bear. David seems to be having a similar internal struggle, from the look on his face when Bo glances over.

When he notices Bo looking, David returns his attention to his plate, his ears going pink. A surge of anticipation cuts through Bo's pie-induced lethargy. The Thanksgiving dinner was a roaring success, despite David's fretting, with enough food, pie, and drinks to feed sixty normal people, so they had plenty for the twenty or so CHL athletes and assorted family members.

The married players with kids are already starting to make noises about it being time to go, even if they aren't quite ready to leave their seats. The younger guys are going to linger for awhile, of course, watching the unlucky assholes who do have games today and going back for seconds on pie and food. But Bo lets himself think ahead to when they're all done. When it's just him, David, and Sasha cleaning up, and they finally manage to get David to understand what they're offering—

"Right?" Dino nudges him in the arm.

"Huh? Sorry, pie coma." Bo refocuses on his current surroundings and allows himself to be drawn into a debate on the best non-hockey sport. Dino argues fervently for soccer, while Harty and Elvis insist it's baseball and Singer shakes off his lethargy and shows his California roots with a treatise on the subtle complexity of surfing that goes on long past the time when everyone else has lost interest.

Bo has long since stopped even pretending to pay attention by the time the last of the families takes their leave. Sasha reluctantly surrenders Alina to her parents—Molly's wife, Ana, holds her hand up and pretends to have her wave goodbye and it's absolutely the cutest thing Bo has ever seen.

As soon as the door closes behind the Yermolayevs, Ads and Rosie make a beeline for the bar, still liberally stocked despite the team's best efforts. "Shots!" Rosie crows, lining up glasses on the counter.

"Three rounds, max," David calls across the room. "And then we start cleaning up before I call a Lyft and send you home. We have a game tomorrow."

"Aye, aye, Cap." Ads shoots off a little salute before he disappears from sight behind the younger players clustering around, leaving David, Sasha, and Bo as the only people left seated.

David glances at them. "You two aren't joining in?"

"Not kid anymore," Sasha says with a shrug. "Can start clean now."

"Nah, they should help." David leans back in his chair, smiling a little as he watches the antics around the bar. "Kind of surprised Mac isn't joining in, though."

Bo rolls his eyes. "I'm setting a good alternate captain example. I thought you'd be happy."

"I am." David turns that fond smile on him. "Just surprised."

"I'm not that bad," Bo protests.

David snorts. "Remind me who had a drinking contest with the rookies?"

"That was two seasons ago! I've matured! Tell him I've matured, Sash."

"Oh yes," Sasha says solemnly, his eyes crinkled at the corners. "Very mature. Goes sleep at 8, wears old man pants."

Bo sighs theatrically. "Betrayed! You can't trust anybody these days."

This time it's David's eyes crinkling with his smile, a smile that has a pleasant warmth settling in Bo's chest. It's almost enough to distract him from his too-full stomach. "I'm proud of you, Mac," David says, captain voice in full force as he claps him on the shoulder. "You're an example to all these young whippersnappers. If only they'd eat three plates of dinner and two pieces of pie like you instead of doing shots."

"I choose to believe you mean that sincerely," Bo says loftily, leaning back in his chair. David's hand lingers on his shoulder, and he can't help but see that as a hopeful sign. It makes him impatient to get the last of the team out of here, so it can be just the three of them. "All right, assholes, that's three rounds. Come on, you heard the captain. Time to clean this shit up."

With eleven other sets of hands to help, all David, Bo, and Sasha have to do is supervise. In a matter of minutes the dirty dishes, silverware, and linens are stacked somewhat neatly in the containers provided by the catering company. There's a surprisingly large number of leftovers, but David produces plastic containers from somewhere and each of the players gets to load up a couple to take home—Bo makes sure to get a slice of coconut cream pie for Sasha and one of key lime for himself before the locust-swarm wipes it all out.

It's all incredibly efficient, as usual when David is organizing something. By the time Parks and Baldy are done negotiating over the last of the stuffing and the final slice of chocolate pecan pie, the Lyfts David ordered are outside waiting. But then there has to be a round of hugs, like they're not going to see each other in the morning at the airport, like they're not going to be flying to fucking Nashville.

Bo is about to twitch out of his skin by the time

they're all gone, letting the door swing shut practically on Silver's heels. They're great guys, he loves them like family, but he just needs them all to *leave*.

Sasha's hand lands on the back of his neck, squeezing gently. Bo takes a breath, holds it for a few seconds before letting it out. "What else?" he asks turning to David.

David shrugs, heading back toward the living room as they trail along behind him. "Honestly, that's about it. Housekeeping's coming tomorrow while I'm gone, and the catering company's going to pick up all the dishes and shit. I'm just gonna check the score on the Krakens/Selkies game, maybe text Stewart for an update on Michaelson before I head to bed."

And that right there—Bo couldn't have asked for a better opening if he'd created one himself. He exchanges a look with Sasha, just a last check, and moves in a little, backing David up against the back of his giant leather sectional. Out of the corner of his eye he can see Sasha joining him, can feel his presence like they're on the ice together. His heart starts beating faster, he opens his mouth—

And someone groans, the unmistakable sound of vomiting filling the room, followed closely by the unmistakable *smell* of vomit. Both of which are, like, the opposite of sexy.

They turn, almost as one, looking over to where Mal is hunched over, half on the couch, which thankfully remains vomit-free, hands braced on the coffee table.

"Aww, buddy," Bo sighs, backing away and circling around the couch. "Too much pie?"

Mal swallows convulsively. "I, uh, I didn't have pie…"

Now that Bo's looking, Mal's cheeks are awfully flushed, and his eyes look a little glassy. "Where's your thermometer?" Bo asks, glancing up at David.

"I'll go get it."

"'M not sick," Mal mumbles, like he's nine instead of nineteen. "Just ate something, or some shit. 'M fine."

Bo shakes his head and nudges the boy back onto the couch, making room for Sasha to squat down and start cleaning up the pool of vomit. "We'll let the thermometer be the judge of that, kiddo. How long have you been asleep?"

Mal shrugs, shivers moving through his body. "I ate a little, but I wasn't really hungry. Tired. Thought I'd grab a quick nap."

"Stick this under your arm," David orders,

returning with a digital thermometer. "I don't want it in your mouth right now."

"Kay." Mal obeys meekly, still shivering a little as they all wait for the electronic beep.

When it comes and he pulls the thermometer free, Bo has to catch it before he drops it. "Well," Bo says flatly, tilting the thermometer so David and Sasha can see the display."

"101 isn't that bad," Mal argues. "Just a couple degrees above normal. I'll sleep it off."

"You add a degree if it's taken under your arm," David says, nudging him to lie down flat. "So you actually have a 102.9 degree fever. Lie there. I'll get you some Tylenol to bring that down and text Coach to let him know you're not coming with us tomorrow."

Mal does his best to sit back up, but makes no headway against the hand David planted on his chest. "I can play!"

"Not with a fever that high, you can't," Bo says, grabbing the throw blanket David keeps on his couch as Sasha heads for the kitchen and shaking it out before draping it over Mal's legs. "Besides, we don't need the whole team coming down with whatever this is. Rest so you can get better and get back on the ice."

"Need rest," Sasha chimes in, coming back with a small trash can and a bottle each of water and Gatorade. "Here, rinse."

Mal takes the bottle of water sullenly, swishes a little around in his mouth and spits into the trash can. "What am I supposed to do while you guys are gone?"

"I'm betting what you'll mostly do is sleep," Bo says. He's doing his best to keep his tone gentle; it's not Mal's fault that he caught some kind of bug and cockblocked them. But there's no way David is going to send him back to his apartment, to maybe infect Deelio and whoever else. No, David is gonna keep Mal here and ply him with Tylenol and fluids until it's time to leave for the roadie, like the giant mama hen he always pretends he isn't.

That's okay. They can do this another time. Maybe on the roadie. So it's not as easy as Bo thought it would be, but he doesn't mind working for things when they're worth it.

THEY BEAT THE NAGAS—NOT easily, exactly, because Nashville dug in their heels and fucking fought for it. Bo nearly gets a shutout, but the fucking sneaky one Kemp knocks in glove-side halfway through the second isn't enough to counteract the fucking filthy goal Xander scores off Sasha's assist, or the messy shot nobody expects Harty to make.

They're full of energy afterward, riding high on the win and the day of rest for Thanksgiving. After press, nearly the whole team plus staff piles into a couple of vans, heads out to eat and drink and relive the game in excruciatingly minute detail like they won't have tape the next morning.

It feels a lot like Thanksgiving, in a way, Bo thinks as he glances around the bar as he nurses his beer. Like family. The younger guys are clustered together at the edge of the dance floor, eyeing the pretty girls in their short denim skirts and cowboy boots, trying to figure out how to make a move. The coaches and most of the staff bowed out after the first round, but Xander and Jordan are cuddled together in a booth, not an inch of space between them and clearly at least halfway to having their hands down each other's pants.

"Awww, young love," Bo says under his breath, nudging Sasha with his elbow and jerking his chin in their direction.

Sasha snorts. "Not so young."

Bo shrugs, taking another sip of his beer and watching David circulate around, checking in with everybody but slowly, inevitably making his way back to them. "Tonight?"

"Maybe," Sasha says, slinging his arm casually along the back of the booth. "Woman over there watching him."

It takes Bo a minute to figure out what woman Sasha's talking about, but then he sees her. She's in jeans instead of a skirt, tight around a nice pair of legs and tucked into what seems like the required footwear for Nashville. And even someone as gay as Bo can acknowledge that her low-cut top is showcasing a very nice rack.

"I mean, that works too," he says, doing his best to feel as unconcerned as he sounds, watching David come ever closer to her. "The goal is to get him laid, right? Doesn't matter who does it."

Sasha side-eyes him in the way that says he knows Bo is full of shit. "Right."

"She just—do you really think she's David's type?"

"He not going to date," Sasha rumbles, nudging a little closer. "For sex? Maybe."

Bo tries not to pout as he takes a larger drink of his beer. "Whatever."

David stops to say something to Rosie and Silver and the woman makes her move, appearing at his side and putting a hand on his arm, eyelashes fluttering. Bo doesn't really want to watch, but he can't seem to look away.

It only takes a couple of minutes for him to relax into Sasha's side, watching as David politely brushes her off, continuing on his way. It's dumb to feel smug, he knows. It's not like David *knows* that Bo and Sasha are going to try and get him into bed tonight.

He feels smug anyway.

Finally, after what feels like an eternity, David slides into the booth next to him with a sigh.

"The kids okay?" Bo chirps, because as cute as David's mama hen routine is, that's prime material.

"Fuck off," David replies without heat, draining the last of his beer. "Just making sure none of them end up with some girl's dad chasing us to the airport with a shotgun."

Bo pats his shoulder gently. "Such a good mom."

"Leave alone," Sasha rumbles, tapping him on the back of the head.

"Thank you," David says fervently, turning his empty longneck around in his hands.

Sasha nods, reaching around Bo to ruffle David's hair. "Is hard, so many kids. Need nanny."

"Et tu, Ivanov?" David groans, rolling his eyes.

"Sorry," Bo says, mostly sincerely. He slides closer, lets his hand land on David's thigh, a little too high for plausible deniability. "You're just doing your captainly duty, and here we are, chirping you for it instead of helping. Let us make it up to you?"

David's eyes flick between him and Sasha, pupils wide and dark in the dim light of the bar. He opens his mouth—

All three of their heads snap around at the crashing sound from the dance floor, Niki holding up his hands placatingly as some redneck asshole swings wildly at him, a gaggle of girls watching avidly.

"*Ni khuyá sebé*," Sasha curses, bolting out of the booth, Bo and David quick on his heels as they all do their best to get there before Niki fucks up something important.

They divide and conquer—David gets between Niki and the local, talks him down with that fucking charismatic bullshit he doesn't even seem to realize he's doing, while Sasha whisks Niki out of sight and Bo talks to the manager, swearing up and down that nothing else is going to happen and just in case, yes, he's good for any damages, here's a black AmEx.

David spends the rest of their time in the bar playing relationship counselor for Redneck Asshole and his girlfriend, who had been cozying up to Niki to get her boyfriend back for some cheating thing a few months earlier. Bo keeps a watchful eye on the rest of the team, cuts them off before they get sloppy enough to do something stupid and calls Lyfts back to the hotel for them as needed. It's the kind of bullshit that he knew he was signing up for when he got the A, but it's still exhausting.

He falls into his hotel bed hours later, rolls over into Sasha's side, and falls asleep before he can even think about jerking off.

6

SASHA

"You what?" Bo repeats, cocking his head, his mouth curling up at the corners in an incredulous grin.

After living in North America for nearly a decade, Sasha is pretty good at understanding English. Speaking it is harder, even if it's not as hard as he pretends sometimes for the press. It's a lot easier to dodge a dumb question if he can turn a blank look on the reporter until they give up and go away. But even when he's not pretending, it's hard sometimes to find the words. Easier just to let Bo do the talking for both of them when it needs to be done. Sasha will stick to actions.

"I invite David come with us to Mexico," Sasha repeats. "Is bye week. He need relax."

Bo nods, slowly, the smile spreading across his face as he turns more toward Sasha, tucking one leg under himself on the couch. "He definitely does. And there'll be nobody to cockblock us in Mexico. You have the best ideas, babe."

Sasha shrugs, smiling back. "Is your idea. I just, what's word? Adapt."

"Don't play dumb with me, Sashenka," Bo says, climbing into his lap. "I'm not some TSN reporter you can just bat your eyelashes at. You're totally the brains of this relationship."

"I get reward?" Sasha asks coyly, rolling his hips up, grinding his cock against Bo's ass. "Positive reinforcement?"

Bo grinds back down to meet him, getting his hand in Sasha's hair and dragging him in for a quick kiss. "I think we can work something out. Especially if you promise to pack the green swim trunks when we go to Mexico."

"Green ones too tight," Sasha protests, but it's hard to really work up any disagreement with Bo moving slow and filthy like that on top of him.

"Mmm, I disagree," Bo says. "I think they're just tight enough."

Sasha slides his hands down the back of Bo's

sweatpants, smiling when he arches into the touch. "Thought I get reward?"

"Feels like I'm the one getting the reward," Bo laughs, pulling Sasha back in.

Kissing Bo while he's laughing is one of Sasha's favorite things. He sometimes likes to think that he can taste the laughter on his lips, in his mouth, as it vibrates between them. "Bedroom," he groans as he tears his mouth away, surging up off the couch.

Bo squeaks a little at the sudden movement but recovers quickly, wrapping his legs around Sasha's waist. "What're you waiting for, babe? Let's go."

Despite Bo's enthusiastic assent, Sasha can't help worrying, now that it's too late to do anything about it. After the third time he finds himself staring at the ceiling, with Bo snoring softly away next to him, he slips out of bed and into the living room. He can sleep on the plane.

As usual this late at night, there's nothing worth watching on TV and he can't settle on anything on Netflix. He finally turns off the TV and picks up his phone, planning to scroll through Instagram and

Twitter until he's tired enough to sleep, when a text pops up from his cousin Viktor. No words, just a video of his new puppy gnawing on a squeaky toy.

))))))))))))))))))))))), Sasha sends back. *getting much sleep, papa?*

Shhh, Viktor replies. *Kiara's mother keeps asking when we'll give her a grandbaby*

Sasha smiles at his phone, both at the words, and the comfort of using Russian again, like relaxing a muscle he hadn't know he was tensing. *Better start soon, old man.*

Two days older! Viktor replies. *Just wait until this summer, babushka has a lot of things to ask you about. Anyway, why are you awake in the middle of the night in America? Is your big expensive bed too soft?*

Sasha hesitates, but he knows he can trust Viktor not to go blabbing to their mothers or their babushka. *I'm thinking about doing something that's maybe not very smart.*

He can practically hear Viktor's laughter in his ear with the response. *Well, that's nothing new. Why would it keep you up at night this time?*

Bo and I have a friend— Sasha pauses, considers how to phrase things. *We want him to be more than a friend, but I'm afraid we might be pushing him into something he doesn't want.*

I always thought dating men would be more straightforward, Viktor replies. *But seriously, Sashenka, unless you're kidnapping this man and tying him to your bed, I think you're fine. Do you trust him to say no?*

Sasha lets out a breath he hadn't realized he was holding. *Yes.*

Then it's fine. You always did worry too much.

You should know, Sasha sends back. *How many months did it take for you to plan how to propose to Kiara?*

The only response is a selfie of Viktor making a rude gesture at the camera.

Going to bed, Sasha replies. *Long flight with many drinks tomorrow. Give Irina a Kiara for me and tell her I'm sorry she married the lesser cousin.*

This time the gesture is even ruder, and made with both hands. Sasha's honestly kind of impressed that Viktor took the time to learn how to use the timer on his phone camera.

He's smiling as he heads back to bed, slipping between the covers without waking Bo up. When his head hits the pillow, he's half-expecting to lie awake again, but that's the last thought he has until morning.

"Go on, get dessert," Bo urges, leaning across David to grab the dessert menu. "It's bye week, you can have cheesecake if you want it."

"Just because it's bye week doesn't mean our macros go out the window," David protests, turning to Sasha on his other side like he's searching for backup.

Sasha shrugs, leaning in a little, boxing David in between them in the corner booth under the pretense of studying the dessert menu. "I'm want ice cream."

David looks resistant for a minute, but then he sags back against the booth. "Fine. Whatever. But I'm bag skating the hell out of both of you when we get back to practice."

"That's the spirit," Bo says, grinning at Sasha as he slides an arm around David's shoulders. "Just come along for the ride, Cap. I promise we'll show you a good time."

"Promise me you're not going to get me arrested, instead," David grumbles, but Sasha can see him lean into Bo's touch.

Bo laughs, offering his hand with the littlest finger extended. "Pinky swear."

David only rolls his eyes a little when they place their dessert order. They manage to coax him into having a couple of bites each of Bo's cheesecake and Sasha's green tea ice cream, and by the time they pay their bill and slide out of the booth, he's looking more relaxed than Sasha's seen him in weeks, maybe months. This was a good idea.

"Come on," Bo says, towing David out of the restaurant. "We need to get changed before we go out."

David groans, dragging his feet a little. "Do we have to? Why can't we just stay in, relax in the suite? We were out on the boat all day."

"How many chances do we get to go out and have fun without having to babysit the team?" Bo asks, herding them into the elevator. "This is happening, buttercup. Suck it up and deal."

"I'm not gonna win this argument, am I?" David asks as they get off on their floor, trailing behind Bo into their suite.

Sasha shakes his head. "*Nyet.*"

"Fine," David groans, heading off to his room. "But if you're not ready in fifteen, I'm changing into my pajamas and going to bed."

"Aye, aye, Cap'n," Bo calls after him. "You heard the man, Sash, go make yourself pretty."

Sasha throws a mock-pout over his shoulder. "Thought I already pretty."

"Pretti*er*," Bo corrects, rolling his eyes and slapping Sasha on the ass. "Wear those jeans I like; the tight ones."

"I not pack those," Sasha informs him smugly.

Bo just grins back at him. "I know. They're in my suitcase."

"Fine," Sasha sighs, heading for the armoire where they stored their luggage.

"And the red shirt!" Bo calls after him.

"No, no," Bo says when they come out into the living room of the suite to find David sprawled across the couch, watching SportsCenter. "You can't wear that."

David looks down at his button-down and slacks. "What's wrong with this?"

"You look like you're about to do press." Bo shakes his head. "Please tell me you packed one pair of jeans?"

"Uh, yeah?"

Bo sighs gustily, pretending to wipe sweat off

his forehead. "Okay, I can work with that. Go, take that off, put on the jeans. I'll get you a shirt."

"I can pick my own shirt," David protests, turning to Sasha like he thinks it'll actually help.

"Clearly you can't," Bo retorts, already heading back to their bedroom. "Go. Jeans. Now."

Sasha just shakes his head in response to David's pleading look. He knows better than to get in Bo's way when he's like this.

"Fine," David grumbles, shoving to his feet and trudging off to his own room as Sasha takes his place on the couch.

He's back in a matter of minutes, wearing only a pair of jeans, loafers, and a petulant expression. "Hurry up, Mac," he yells when he sees Sasha alone on the couch. "Your fifteen minutes are almost up!"

"I'm coming, keep your shirt on," Bo calls back, coming into the living room with a folded t-shirt in his hands. "Or maybe not. That's a good look on you, Cap. Maybe we should just go like that."

Watching the way his chest flexes as David ducks his head, Sasha has to agree. It's not like he's never seen David without a shirt on; hockey players lose all body consciousness way before they make it to the CHL level. But the locker room is different.

Seeing him like this, half-dressed in a shared living space, feels…intimate.

"Give me the shirt, Mac," David growls, stalking across the room. "Or I'm going to bed and you two can do whatever you're doing without me."

"Fine. Catch." Bo tosses the shirt at him.

David barely catches it before it hits him in the face, shakes it out and pulls it on. "This is too small," he complains as he pushes his arms into the sleeves, tugging the shirt down over his stomach. "Why can't I wear one of my shirts?"

"It's not too small, all of your shirts are too big," Bo retorts. "We're not going to a cotillion or some shit, we're going clubbing. That shirt makes your arms look great, and you're wearing it. End of discussion."

"I'm the captain here," David protests, but weakly, like he knows a losing battle when he sees one.

Bo shakes his head and turns toward the door. "We're on vacation. Come on, let's go."

"Does he boss you around like that in bed?" David mutters to Sasha, his face going pinker almost immediately. "Shit, forget I said that."

"Sometimes," Sasha says quietly as he brushes past David on his way to the door. "Coming?"

He misses whatever reply David might have made when Bo grabs his ass on the way into the elevator.

SASHA IS FAIRLY sure that Bo chose this resort because it had the nightclub on the grounds, so they don't have to worry about transportation. A short elevator ride, an even shorter walk, and they're walking into the dimly lit space. It's surprisingly crowded, considering it's not even ten yet, but Bo must have called ahead, because after a short conversation with the hostess they're shown to a corner booth next to the dance floor.

"What can I get you gentlemen?" the hostess asks, whisking away the "Reserved" sign from the tabletop.

"Two rounds of tequila shots, please," Bo requests, gesturing David into the booth ahead of him and handing over his credit card. "Can we start a tab?"

She returns his smile, hers carefully calculated to be warm and friendly but not inviting. It's impressive. "Certainly sir. Someone will be right out with those."

True to her word, only a few minutes after she disappears, an attractive young man carries a tray of shot glasses, lime wedges, and salt shakers to their table, sliding it toward them with expert precision. "Two rounds of tequila shots. Can I get you anything else?"

"Not right now," Bo says, pulling the tray a little closer. "Thanks."

"Tequila shots?" David asks, eyeing the tray dubiously. "We're not college kids on spring break, Mac."

Bo picks up the salt shaker, grinning. "No, but we are in Mexico. You don't have to if you don't want to."

"It's fine, but I'm having beer after—"

David's voice cuts off abruptly when Bo picks up his hand.

"This okay?"

David nods silently, watching as Bo licks slowly over the skin between his thumb and forefinger, holding eye contact while he sprinkles the salt over it. Tucking a lime wedge into David's loosely curled fingers, he licks the salt off his skin, throws back the shot, and closes his mouth over David's fingers before sinking his teeth into the lime.

Sasha watches David's throat work, the way he

can't look away from Bo's mouth. As soon as David's fingers slip free from Bo's mouth, Sasha takes his other hand. "Okay?" he asks, as quietly as he can and still be heard over the pounding bass.

He waits for a nod before bending his head, keeping eye contact. David's skin is warm under his tongue, the salt from the shaker mixing with the lingering taste of sweat. Sasha throws back the shot, lets his tongue linger on David's fingers before biting down on the lime and letting the sour juice chase the burn of the tequila.

David's teeth sink into his lower lip as he reaches for a salt-shaker. He hesitates for a minute, then pulls Sasha's hand toward him, licks over the skin and sprinkles the salt. The second drag of his tongue is even slower, makes the skin on Sasha's hand feel like it's wired directly to his cock. By the time David sucks the lime wedge from between his fingertips, he's at least half hard in his jeans.

Watching David lick Bo's hand, the line of his throat working as he throws back the shot, the pink flash of his tongue as he sucks on the wedge, gets him the rest of the way there. Bo takes his second shot, and Sasha does his on autopilot before pulling David out of the booth. "Come. Dance."

David goes willingly, comes into his arms and

starts to move with him to the music, one hand resting on Sasha's hip, one on his shoulder. After a few minutes of this, though, he pulls Sasha's head down to speak in his ear. "What're we doing here, Sash?"

"Dancing," Sasha replies, pretending not to understand. He turns David around, pulls him in until they're plastered together, David's back to his chest, no space between them. Leans down until his lips are brushing David's ear. "Look. Bo watching."

He feels David's ribcage expand with the breath he sucks in. Bo is, in fact, watching them, hand wrapped loosely around a bottle of beer he's ignoring in favor of devouring them with his eyes.

Sasha half-expects David to bolt, now that their intentions are out in the open. Either that or take a step back, explain in his captain voice whatever dumb reason he has for thinking it's a bad idea.

What he doesn't expect is for David to melt against him, tipping his head back on Sasha's shoulder and turning until he can say, "Let's give him a show, then," directly into Sasha's ear.

The song changes then, something with a slow, driving beat that feels like sex. David reaches up to curl a hand around the back of Sasha's neck, grinds his ass back against Sasha's cock like there's nothing there but skin on skin. It's all Sasha can do to maintain a grip on his hips, thumbs slipping under the space where his t-shirt meets his jeans. He can feel the shiver slide through David's body like it's his own, they're pressed together so tightly.

It only takes the length of one endless song before Bo pushes to his feet and stalks across the dance floor toward them. Sasha is almost pathetically grateful; he can't guarantee that he won't come in his pants if David keeps this up for much longer.

Instead of dragging them off the dance floor like Sasha's hoping, Bo just slides into David's space, one hand slotting in above Sasha's on his waist, the other curling around Sasha's bicep. He fits his movements to their seamlessly and Sasha can't help but groan when David presses back even harder against him, more delicious friction on his cock.

It's instinctive to lean down when Bo tilts his face up, to meet him for a kiss that maybe crosses the line a little for what's appropriate in public. It's familiar, the shape and the taste of Bo's kiss, but new, too, thanks to the solid warmth of David's body between them, the catch in his breath where it hits Sasha's cheek.

Bo pulls back eventually, when they're both breathing hard, but he doesn't go far, just turns his face toward David's. They stay like that for an endless moment, inches apart.

Sasha isn't sure who moves first. One moment they're staring into each other's eyes, the next they're kissing, hot and wet and hungry. And Sasha has a front-row seat. He's not entirely sure what he did to deserve this, if it was good or evil, but whatever it was, he doesn't intend to miss a minute of it.

They finally break apart, David's head falling back onto Sasha's shoulder as he gasps for breath. Bo takes the opportunity to nip at his neck, scraping teeth down to where his traps rise up out of his shirt. David groans softly, something more heard than felt. He looks wrecked already, his lips wet and red where they part over his teeth, eyes wide and dark in the dim light.

Sasha leans in, capturing those lips with his own. It's an awkward, shallow angle, given their position, but still so good, like sparks moving through him from every place David and Bo are touching him.

"Fuck, that's hot," Bo says when they finally part, still so close that they can hear him easily. "Wanna take this someplace more private?"

"*Da*," Sasha says emphatically. "Good plan."

Bo leans in for one last, quick kiss. "You know I make the best plans, babe. Come on, let's go."

Sasha misses the warmth of David's body against his almost immediately, but at least the cool air and lack of friction have a slight calming effect on his overeager cock. Following Bo and David out of the club still isn't exactly what he'd call comfortable, though.

They make their way to the elevator in silence, carefully not touching. Sasha can't help feeling a little surprised at Bo's forbearance, but it's for the best. The last thing they need is some cell phone photo or, God forbid, video of the three of them making out in a resort elevator, articles about public indecency and the CHL party lifestyle splashed across the internet.

They travel up to their floor in electric, anticipatory silence, eyes meeting and then flicking away, hands flexing at their sides. The ding of the elevator as it stops makes them all jump a little, laugh a little. Sasha has no idea how long it takes to walk from the elevator to their suite, only that they're suddenly there, the door swinging closed behind them, leaving them in privacy at last.

The only light on is the small fixture by the door, warm and golden against the cooler light filtering in through the plate-glass windows. The room feels small, intimate, no bigger than the space needed for them to stand, bare inches apart. Someone is going to have to move, to speak, to break the spell. But this seems like a moment that needs words, so Sasha meets Bo's eyes, nods.

Bo reaches out a hand toward David. "Stay with us?"

7

DAVID

David should have known better than to agree to this vacation—although, thinking back, he's not entirely sure he did agree. He's not sure Sasha even asked, just assumed that David would come with them. And David never has been able to keep from torturing himself with their presence.

But this—this is a whole new level. The boat was bad enough—Sasha in a pair of green swim trunks that hugged his ass lovingly and left his dick print clearly fucking visible, while Bo lounged around in a pair of tiny, even tighter shorts that looked more like compression gear than anything for swimming. Then dinner, boxed in between them in the tiny booth and trying hard to remember why that was a bad thing when they fed him bites of their dessert and then licked the fork or spoon clean after, like they were searching for the taste of his mouth.

At this point, he's pretty sure he's about to die from lack of blood to his brain. Everything after the restaurant feels like some kind of strange dream. Bo's slow, appreciative look at his bare chest. Wearing a shirt scented with a mixture of Sasha's aftershave and Bo's cologne. Their hands, their tongues on his skin, his fingertips—people have done body shots off his abs that felt less intimate than those shots, and all they touched were his hands.

By the time they made it to the dance floor, he was half-convinced that he was actually dreaming. There was no way that he was grinding with Sasha in the middle of a crowded club, Bo's eyes hot and intent on them. No way he was pinned between Bo and Sasha as they kissed, no way they each kissed him with equal hunger.

He can't even resent them for doing it, for riding the wave of tequila and the almost palpable air of horniness that permeated the club. It was absolutely the hottest encounter he's had in recent memory, and he does his best to remember it that way, not to focus on the hollow ache in his chest now that he's not touching them.

He's going to have jerk-off material for months, maybe years, and his cock is very excited about the prospect of getting started with that promptly, regardless of how he might be feeling emotionally. He's just opening his mouth to excuse himself, to try—and fail—not to imagine what they might be getting up to in their room, when Bo holds out a hand.

"Stay with us?"

David knows—he knows this is a dumb idea. But standing here in the dimly lit room, with their eyes hot on him, he can't bring himself to say no. It's not like it's the first time in his life he's done something stupid, and it sure as shit won't be the last. Faced with a chance to get what he wants, even just a taste of it, there's only one answer he can give.

"Okay," he says softly, taking Bo's hand and letting himself be pulled in.

"Fuck yeah," Bo breathes.

Kissing Bo is even better like this, in the dim room with only Sasha to see. Bo's mouth is just as hungry and greedy as his hands, roaming over David's body, sliding under his shirt and as far into his jeans as possible, flicking at his nipple, squeezing his ass until David whines into the kiss.

David never wants it to end, but eventually he has to breathe. "Fuck," he whispers, flexing his fingers where they somehow ended up on Bo's hips. "What—what are we doing here?"

"I feel like you've had sex before," Bo laughs, pushing his shirt up. "But if not, I can probably walk you through it."

"He like to talk," Sasha rumbles from behind him, the only warning David gets before there's another set of hands on him, helping Bo get his shirt up and over his head.

David shivers at the feeling when their hands come back, pulling him back against Sasha's broad chest. "What a surprise."

He jolts when Bo pinches his nipple lightly, heat flashing through his body. "Smartass," Bo says. His voice is fond, though. "What do you say we relocate this to the bedroom so we don't have to explain to any of the trainers how we injured ourselves on vacation?"

"Best plans," Sasha agrees, nudging them toward the bedroom door.

"I'm not gonna be the only one getting naked," David says, but lets himself be moved, walked into the bedroom with their hands still warm on his skin.

Then Sasha's kissing him. Fuck, it's even better than he'd imagined, pressed up against that big, solid body, the soft fabric of Sasha's shirt rasping lightly against his nipples where they're already so hard and sensitive. Bo moves in behind him and David makes a truly embarrassing noise. Being boxed in between them right now, pinned between their bodies, is more intense than it was on the dance floor, because now it's not a tease, a joke, blowing off steam. They're really doing this.

"Fuck," he breathes again when Sasha lifts his head. Somehow his hands wound up under Sasha's shirt, rucking it up to find skin, so he pushes it higher. "Come on, Sash. Get this off."

"Trade," Sasha says, smirking down at him. "My shirt, your pants."

David laughs, surprising himself. "How about my pants for your shirt and Mac's?"

"You know my name," Bo breathes, nipping at his earlobe, hands sliding around David's stomach to find the button on his jeans. "C'mon, David."

"Bo," David said, letting himself taste the name on his tongue, allowing himself that intimacy. "Take your fucking shirt off."

Bo laughs in his ear before pulling back a little. "Aye, aye, Cap'n."

And yeah, David misses the warmth of Bo's body against his back, but taking a step back to watch Bo and Sasha strip their shirts off is good, too. Miles and miles of skin and flexing muscle on display, and he starts to look away reflexively before he remembers that he doesn't have to. He can look. He can touch. He's going to touch.

"We had a deal," Bo says when his shirt is off, reaching out to run a hand down David's chest. "Do I get to take your pants off now?"

"Be my guest," David says, surprising himself a little. "I'm beginning to think maybe I got the short end of the stick, here."

Bo laughed, undoing the button on his jeans and pulling the zipper slowly down. "Nah, everybody's getting naked here. Don't worry. Let us take care of you, huh?"

And fuck, that sounds just…so fucking tempting. David lets himself lean into Bo's space, just a little, lets himself watch as Bo slides to his knees, pulling his jeans and boxers along with them. And then he just…stays there, running his hands up and down David's thighs, like David's stupid cock isn't right there, hard and heavy and rising toward his stomach with every pulse of blood through his body.

"You like that?" Sasha rumbles from behind him, a second before his hands land on David's hips. "He look good on knees, no?"

"Yes," David manages to get the word out somehow, through a throat gone dry.

Bo smirks up at him, licks his lips like the provocative asshole he is. "Yes to which, David?"

"Yes to both, jackass," David retorts reflexively, then immediately bites his tongue.

But Bo just smiles up at him, laughing a little, and Sasha moves further into his space. Apparently he found time to remove his jeans beforehand, since there's only soft fabric between David's ass and the hard, hot line of Sasha's cock, pressing urgently against him.

"What do you want?" Bo asks, his hands still following their slow, maddening path, up and down, up and down. "Whatever you want, David."

"I—" he stumbles to a stop. What does he want? His head swims with ideas, fantasies, mental pictures, coming so quickly that he can't separate one from another. "I—I have no fucking clue."

Their hands on him are the only thing keeping him from making a break for it, hiding in his room until he can't avoid them any more. He can feel the heat in his face, his neck, crawling down his chest, and he can't quite manage to meet Bo's eyes.

"That's okay," Bo says, so close now that David can feel his breath on his cock.

"Let us take care," Sasha agrees, lips brushing David's ear. "Okay?"

David nods, letting his head fall back onto Sasha's shoulder, his eyes sliding closed. "Okay," he agrees.

He shivers as Bo's hands move up higher, thumbs following the cut of his hips, then back down. One of them finally, finally curls around the root of his cock, giving it one long, slow stroke. It's so simple, so basic, someone's hands on him, but so good he's suddenly weak at the knees. Sasha's hands, Sasha's solid warmth are the only things holding him upright.

When Bo's mouth closes over him, he can't stop the moan that slips out of his mouth. "Fuck, Bo—fuck."

"He good with mouth," Sasha murmurs in his ear, one hand sliding slowly up David's chest.

David would laugh at the understatement if he wasn't currently preoccupied with trying not to come embarrassingly fast. "Y-yeah."

Sasha licks at the shell of his ear, his tongue a shockingly erotic counterpoint to the lush, wet heat of Bo's mouth. "Want fuck you," he breathes, his thumb grazing lightly over David's nipple like he knows exactly how sensitive it is. "Okay?"

"Fuck, yes," David blurts out. Right now that sounds like the best idea he's ever heard. "Yeah, please—"

"We've got you," Bo soothes, pulling back but keeping his hands on David's skin, warm and grounding. "C'mon, let's get to the bed."

They coax him toward the bed, nudging him down to sit on the edge. "So," Bo says, unbuttoning his jeans and stripping them off, his boxer briefs following them to the floor in short order. "We don't have to do anything elaborate. I can watch Sash fuck you and jerk off."

"Or?"

"Or," Bo echoes, closing the space between them as Sasha tosses his own jeans to the side. "I've been thinking about you fucking me while Sasha fucks you for like, months. Only if you want to, though, no pressure—"

David reaches up, stops the flood of babble by pressing his fingers to Bo's lips. "Yes."

"Yeah?" Bo blinks down at him. "Really?"

"No, I'm just fucking with you." David rolls his eyes. "If you seriously think I'd say no to an offer like that, you're crazier than any goalie I've ever met."

He probably shouldn't find Bo's little victory shimmy as adorable as he does. Gotta blame it on lack of blood flow. Right.

"So how are we doing this?" he asks, doing his best to divert his mind from the danger zone.

Bo crawls up onto the bed, making a show of it, because of course he does. David can't bring himself to mind, though—it's a damn good show. Sasha seems to agree, his expression a mixture of desire and affection as he watches Bo lean over to dig something out of the little bedside table and settle back against the pillows.

"That's up to you," Bo says, drawing his knees up, feet resting flat against the bed. His abs ripple as he lifts his hips, shoving a pillow under them with the hand not holding the lube. "Do you wanna open me up? Or watch me do it while Sash preps you? Not gonna lie, I think I'd enjoy the first one more, but if you think you'll get distracted—"

"I'm a professional athlete," David shoots back, unable to stop himself even though he knows Bo is baiting him on purpose. "I think I can focus on one simple task."

Bo grins. "If you say so. You've never tried to focus with Sasha's fingers inside you. But you can let me know if you need to tap out. No shame in it."

"Give me that," David grumbled, crawling up on the bed and holding out his hand for the lube. "Tap out. What the fuck, man?"

"Stop teasing David," Sasha says mildly, the mattress shifting under his weight as he joins them. "Not nice."

Whatever Bo was going to answer is lost in the yelp as David drizzles the lube directly onto him, without bothering to warm it first. "Jesus! You could warn a guy."

"You could not dare me," David returns, teasing a finger over the pucker of muscle. "Isn't that a fine-able offense?"

"Well, first, we're on vacation—" Bo sucks in a breath as David presses lightly, just another tease, except his fingertip slips just inside. "And secondly, I never said the word 'dare.' Sash'll be my witness, won't you Sashenka?"

Sasha laughs, stroking a hand down David's back. "Was distracted. Not sure."

Bo attempts to pout, but the effect is ruined

when his mouth falls open as David thrusts his finger deeper and deeper. "Fuck," he groans, letting his head sink back against the pillows. "Maybe—maybe we cancel the snark and get to the fucking? I'm not gonna need much prep."

"This doesn't feel like fucking?" David asks mildly, adding more lube and a second finger. It's kind of incredible, the way Bo's body just opens for him. It takes every ounce of self-control he has not to rush it, to push his way inside and see if Bo will open for his cock the same way.

He's so occupied with his task, the way Bo's body moves under his hands, the little sounds he makes, the way he lifts his hips, fucking himself on David's fingers, that he doesn't even realize the lube has disappeared from where he left it. It's only when Sasha's hand lands on his back, urging him to bend forward a little more, that he remembers the other part of tonight's agenda.

The first brush of Sasha's finger against his ass is almost startling, even though he expected it. But then, it's been a few months since he's had anything there but his own fingers. It takes him a minute to remember how to breathe, to bear down and accept the intrusion. Especially since he is actually a little distracted, dammit. But he defies any human being not to be distracted by the sight of Bo writhing, taking three fingers and seemingly on the verge of begging for more.

"I'm ready," Bo pants, his whole body moving in long, liquid rolls to meet every thrust of David's fingers. "C'mon, I'm ready. Sash, tell him."

When David turns his head to look over his shoulder, Sasha shrugs, never stopping his own movements. "Always say that. But he like tease, if you want."

"Fucker, no I fucking don't." Bo turns a pleading look on David. "I like getting fucked. Come on, get a condom and get in me. I'm so ready, I bet you can just shove right in. Come on, I'm ready, please."

"Well," David pretends to consider it, like his cock isn't screaming at him to do it, to get inside that tight, wet heat. "I guess you did ask nicely."

Bo lets out a long, shuddering exhale. "Fuck yeah, I did. C'mon, condom's right there, don't leave me hanging—"

"Is he always this bossy?" David asks over his shoulder, grabbing the condom with his clean hand.

"*Nyet,*" Sasha said, grazing David's prostate and lighting him up like a Christmas tree. "Usually worse."

David shakes his head, tearing the foil packet open with his teeth and rolling the latex on carefully. Even that much touch is almost unbearably good, after so long with nobody and nothing touching his cock. "Man, I don't know how you put up with him. Is he really that good a lay?"

"Get the fuck inside me and find out," Bo practically growls, hooking a heel around the back of David's thigh and dragging him closer. "I swear to fucking—"

As it turns out, David actually can just push inside, bottoming out in one long, slick thrust, which has the beneficial side effect of temporarily shutting Bo up. It feels so amazing that he has to pause, frozen just like that, knowing it will be even better if he moves, but unable to make himself pull out just yet, to leave .

"Yesss," Bo hisses, his eyes fluttering shut. "God, come on, fuck me, already."

"Bossy," David says again, shaking his head and trying to find his focus. He can't quite manage the casual tone he's going for, not with the hot, tight squeeze of Bo's ass around him, the smooth, relentless thrusts of Sasha's fingers inside him. "I need a minute. Unless you want me to go off in like thirty seconds and leave you to get yourself off."

Bo grins up at him, wrapping a leg around his waist. "I mean, that would definitely be hot. And I bet you could get it up again."

"I don't know what kind of fantasy world you're living in—" David loses his words as Bo starts to move under him, body rolling as he, Jesus fuck, fucks himself deeper on David's cock

Sasha adds another finger, the stretch serious enough that it keeps him from embarrassing himself like a teenager with a hair-trigger, thank goodness. He finally gets enough focus back to start moving, slow, shallow thrusts, matching Bo's rhythm instinctively.

"Oh, yeah," Bo groans. "Knew you'd be good at this. C'mon, Sash, quit stalling and get with the program or I'm gonna come before you even get it in."

"Yeah," David agrees, a little breathless and a lot sure he can't take much more of Sasha's skilled fingers without losing it. "Come on, I'm ready."

Sasha hums, considering, but after a few seconds he pulls his fingers free with one last torturous drag of his fingertips over David's prostate as a parting shot. It's distracting enough that David almost misses the sound of the condom packet. Then suddenly Sasha is right there, closer than before, one big hand pressing on the small of his back, bending him over until he's on his hands and knees.

He braces himself with one hand next to Bo's shoulder. "Hi," he says inanely, trying not to focus on the hands spreading him wide, the blunt pressure against his ass.

"Hi," Bo says back, curling a hand around the back of his neck and pulling him down for a kiss, wet and open and distracting.

David has to break free and pant for breath as Sasha pushes slowly, inexorably inside. The stretch is incredible, just this side of too much even with the prep. But the most overwhelming thing is the sensation of being surrounded by them, their hands on his skin, their bodies sheltering him. It's so much more than he ever imagined; for a moment he feels like all it would take would be one of them breathing on him to make him combust, shatter him into a million pieces.

"Okay?" Sasha murmurs, one arm sliding around him to press against his chest, hand landing over his heart.

"Yeah," David manages to get out. "Yeah, I—yeah."

Bo runs soothing hands up his arms, fingers curling around his biceps. "Need a minute?"

"Maybe."

They stay like that for an endless, suspended moment, until he feels less like they're going to destroy him. An experimental thrust into Bo proves that he has just enough room between them to move a little. "Okay," he gasps when Sasha follows his movement. "I—yeah."

"Fuck yeah," Bo laughs, arching his head back onto the pillow as they begin to move in earnest. "Let's do this."

He yelps when Sasha drops a hand to his chest, tweaking one of his nipples harder than David would dare to, tightening convulsively around David's cock. "Hey!"

"Quiet," Sasha rumbles, his other hand coming down to rest on David's hip. "Got two men fuck you. Should be grateful."

"Oh, Sashenka, baby, I am so fucking—" his fingers tighten on David's arms, digging in to the muscle "—grateful. Gonna show you later. If I can walk after this."

Sasha nips at David's ear. "Sounds like challenge."

"Yeah," David agrees, which is about all his

brain cells can up with at the moment, considering the distinct lack of blood flow they're dealing with.

He lets Sasha guide his free hand down to Bo's nipple, squeeze his fingers together to pinch it tightly. Bo's whole body jolts at the touch and Sasha rumbles approvingly, leaving David to continue as he turns his attention to fucking both of them into oblivion.

Normally David prides himself on being an active, attentive lover, but all he can do right now is hold on. Sasha's relentless, measured thrusts push him into Bo, over and over. The duality of the sensation, fucking and being fucked, the tight clutch of Bo's ass around him, the hot, thick slide of Sasha's cock into him, builds David's orgasm higher and higher until he's not sure anymore who's moving faster, him or Sasha. All he knows is that they're speeding up, harder and faster, an almost brutal pace until he comes, his orgasm almost wrenched out of him as he shoves, hard and grace-less, inside Bo one, two more times before he goes still.

Sasha fucks him mercilessly through it, hands in a vice-like grip on his hips. Once David's recovered enough to see again, he's greeted by the sight of Bo writhing under him, one hand stripping his cock as

Sasha's thrusts fuck David into him. It probably shouldn't be this hot, Sasha using him to fuck Bo, but David can't fight the shudder that rips through him at the thought, almost strong enough to be another little orgasm.

He finally recovers enough brain function to get his hand on Bo's nipple again, scraping a nail over it before pinching. Bo comes with a groan, his ass flexing around David's cock hard enough to wring another aftershock out of him. Behind him, Sasha finally loses his rhythm, slamming in deep one last time, biting down on David's trap as he goes still.

They stay like that until David can feel sweat rising everywhere they're pressed together, but he still doesn't want to move, to leave this moment where he's blanketed by their bodies. Eventually though, Sasha straightens, kissing the bite marks on David's shoulder as he pulls carefully out.

"Ugh," Bo complains when David follows suit. "That was too hot. I'm dead. RIP me."

"Is very sad," Sasha agrees solemnly, climbing down off the bed and heading for their bathroom. "Will be missed."

David hesitates for a moment before also leaving the bed, carefully slipping the condom off and tying it in a knot. If there was any justice in the world, he would've had to search for a trash can, giving him a chance to figure out how to play this. But of course they're staying at a luxury resort hotel with a trash can right next to the fucking bed.

"Come cuddle," Bo says plaintively, making grabby hands in his direction before he can hesitate too long. "I'm a needy little monster after sex, just ask Sash."

"Is true," Sasha confirms, returning from the bathroom and handing David a warm washcloth, nudging him toward the bed. "Very needy. One man not enough."

No matter how much part of David is screaming at him to get out of there, he's not that big of an asshole. So he lets himself be urged back onto the bed, wipes the sticky mess off Bo's abs and then, after a moment of hesitation, between his legs. He jumps a little when Sasha does the same for him, but tries not to think too hard about it. About the way Sasha takes both soiled cloths away while Bo pulls him down for remarkably aggressive cuddles. About Sasha coming back from the bathroom and turning off the lamp, sliding into the bed behind David and slinging an arm over his waist.

"Sleep," Sasha rumbles.

Bo nods against David's shoulder. "Sleep."

David's brain is screaming at him that this is a bad idea, that he needs to get out, but his stupid, stupid body is already halfway to sleep, relaxed and warm and content in a way it hasn't been in months.

Tomorrow, he thinks drowsily, already slipping into sleep. *Worry about it tomorrow.*

8

BO

I make the best plans, Bo thinks as he drifts awake, his head pillowed on David's shoulder. The angle of the sun says they slept in a little more than they're used to, but they also stayed up God knows how late last night. Totally worth it, though.

Despite the warning numbness in the arm stuck under him, ready to spring into pins and needles as soon as the blood flow comes rushing back, Bo doesn't really want to move. When he blinks his eyes open he can see Sasha on the other side of David, still snoring softly, His hair is it's usual morning rat's nest and he's got one arm slung across David's stomach, fingertips brushing possessively over Bo's hip even in his sleep.

David looks younger in sleep. It's such a cliche thing, but he does. Aside from last night, Bo can't think of a time he's seen David forget about the team, all the captain shit, everything that comes with being a CHL player, and just *be*. But like this, his face soft in the morning light, without the mantle of authority he wears like his skin—yeah.

Before Bo can get too embarrassed by his sappiness, though, David's lashes start to flutter, his breathing changing as he wakes up.

"Hey," Bo says softly, even though he knows damn well that Sasha could sleep through an earthquake if he wasn't ready to wake up.

David clears his throat, his eyes still fuzzy with sleep. "Hey."

He's so fucking cute like this that Bo can't help but grin. "Okay, the way I see it, we have a couple of options here. At least."

"Okay?" David shivers a little when Bo presses a kiss to his collarbone. "Mac—Bo—what—Sasha's right—"

"Trust me when I say that no force on earth will wake that man up if he's not ready to," Bo interrupts, shifting closer as his mouth moves higher. He rubs his morning wood shamelessly against David's hip, groaning a little. "He has literally slept through a blowjob before, okay?"

David blinks at him. "Really?"

"The whole goddamn thing, swallowing and all," Bo confirms. He has to basically drape himself over David's body to kiss under his ear, at the hinge of his jaw, but that isn't exactly a hardship. Especially when David's hands come up to his waist, nudging him down the necessary inch or two for their cocks to line up. "Fuck."

"Yeah," David gasps, his hips hitching up. And that's even better, the movement, even though it's too dry, really.

Bo allows himself a couple more seconds to savor it before he lifts up. "Look, as good as that feels right now, I don't really feel like walking around with a chafed cock for the next week and a half."

"Where did we put the lube?" David lifts his head as much as he can, craning his neck to look around.

"I have a better idea," Bo says, sliding down his body with a wicked grin, leaving a trail of kisses and licks as he goes.

David stares at him, either unbelieving or still too asleep to realize what Bo is aiming for. His head falls back down onto the pillow as Bo licks up his shaft, circling the head with his tongue before taking it inside.

"Fuck," David groans, his hands hovering above Bo's shoulders like he's not sure where to put them. "Jesus fuck. You're good at that.

Bo lifts up long enough to reach for David's hands, bring them to his head. "You can pull my hair a little. If you want."

"I—you—fuck." David lifts up enough to grab a pillow and shove it under his head. "Really?"

"Really. I like it. You can ask Sash when he wakes up."

Bo turns his attention back to the task at hand, moaning a little when David tugs tentatively at his hair. It's barely anything, but it still has him lighting up, like sparks dancing over his skin. He redoubles his efforts, sliding down until his nose is nearly brushing the neatly trimmed curls at the base of David's cock.

"Oh fuck," David groans, his fingers tightening reflexively. "Fuck, you—I'm not gonna last long —shit, fuck—"

This is Bo's favorite part of blowjobs, honestly. He likes the physical sensations, the weight of a cock in his mouth, the bright sting of a hand in his hair, the challenge of mastering his gag reflex. But he's never really gotten over the feeling of power, taking a man apart with nothing but his lips and tongue and the slightest edge of teeth.

He's so caught up in it, in learning what makes David shake and curse and groan, that he almost misses the shifting next to them. He definitely doesn't miss the sound of the lube clicking open, or the slick sounds as Sasha starts to stroke his cock.

It takes David a little longer, but, to be fair, he's more distracted. As soon as he realizes, though, his hands fall away, his hips hitching up at the involuntary noise Bo makes around his cock. "I—we can stop—"

"*Nyet*," Sasha rasps, his hand moving faster over his cock. He reaches out with his free hand, lifting David's hand back to Bo's hair, holding it there until he takes a tentative grip. "Is hot. Want watch."

"Fuck," David's hands are still a little tentative, but his cock twitches a little against Bo's tongue, a bitter drop of precome working its way free. "I—really?"

Sasha gives him his most unimpressed bitchface expression, the one that would make Bo laugh if he didn't have a mouthful of cock right now. Instead he redoubles his efforts, pulling out every trick he knows to see which ones work on David. In a grati-fyingly short time, he has both of David's hands back in his hair, David choking out a warning and trying to pull him off.

Despite his best efforts, Bo refuses to be moved, pulling back against David's hands and sucking on the head as he comes, filling his mouth. Bo swal-lows every last drop, sucking gently until David uses his grip on his hair to tug him upward, shuddering with the sensation even once Bo's mouth leaves his skin.

Next to them, Sasha growls, reaching out to curl a hand around the back of Bo's neck and pull him up for a kiss. He licks into Bo's mouth like he's trying to chase down every last taste of David's semen. It's so incredibly, unbearably hot that Bo grinds helplessly against his hip, desperately chasing an orgasm that suddenly feels impossibly close.

Sasha groans into his mouth and comes, hot and wet all over Bo's stomach. Bo follows him seconds later, nearly overbalancing with the force of his orgasm until David's hand steadies him, warm and sure on the small of his back.

"Fuck," Bo breathes when he can finally get air back in his lungs. He rolls onto his back and collapses heedlessly, landing more or less halfway on both David and Sasha. "I make the best plans."

"I want to argue with that on principle," David says, wriggling to the side to make room for him. "Give me a second to get blood flow back to my brain."

Sasha shakes his head, rolling off the bed and dragging both of them after him. "No, no argue. Shower. Breakfast."

"So bossy," Bo complains, but shower and breakfast sound pretty good, so he follows along as best he can on legs still rubbery.

"Okay," he admits after a few minutes under the spray. The shower is massive, but none of them are entirely small, so there's enough bumping and sliding together that he'd be hard in under 30 seconds if he hadn't just come. "This was a good idea."

"Best plans," Sasha says smugly.

The squeaking yelp he makes when David and Bo splash water in his face simultaneously is really satisfying.

THEIR LAST DAY in Mexico passes in a blur of food,

naps, and more sex than Bo had really thought it was possible to have in that short of a time. But watching David doze off on the plane home, his shoulders loose and relaxed like they haven't been in months, maybe ever, is completely worth it.

Bo snorts out a laugh and closes his own eyes. Yeah. Super-hot marathon sex with his boyfriend and their best friend. Such a fucking hardship.

"I'm a genius," he crows to Sasha once they've dropped David off at his place. Which, sure, that's not exactly the ideal situation, but he probably just wants to get some actual sleep. God knows they hadn't really been able to keep their hands off each other for the entire vacation, but they're back home, and they have practice tomorrow.

"Yes, yes, I know," Sasha grumbles, unlocking the apartment and dropping their bags just inside. He kicks out of his shoes and heads straight for the bedroom, stripping as he goes, not bothering to turn on the lights. "Need sleep. Genius plan make me tired."

Locking the door behind them, Bo shrugs and follows suit. "Yeah, me too. No offense, babe, but I'm pretty sure I couldn't get it up with a crane and a truckload of Viagra."

"*Da*," Sasha agrees, face-planting onto their bed. "Sleep."

"You know you're gonna get cold halfway through the night if you don't get under the covers," Bo mumbles as he shoves his sweatpants and underwear to the floor, his jaw cracking on a yawn.

Sasha groans into the duvet, smooth and clean from the housekeeping service that had visited while they were gone. The light of the setting sun sneaks through a tiny gap in the curtain, lighting his hair with red-gold. "*Nyet*. Sleep."

"Come on, Sashenka," Bo cajoles. Tugging the duvet down with Sasha's weight on top of it is tricky, and he's more than half-tempted to use it to dump his stubborn boyfriend onto the floor. "Nice soft blanket on top of you. And we can cuddle."

"Ugh," Sasha groans again, but he lifts up enough to let Bo maneuver the duvet out from under him and spread it over both of them.

Another yawn overtakes him before he can say anything, missed hours of sleep catching up with him all at once. Exhaustion presses him into the mattress with an almost physical weight.

Anything else he has to say can wait until morning.

BY THE TIME they make it off the ice after practice, Bo feels like he's been hit by a truck. If anything, David pushed them even harder than before Mexico, no sign in his face of the soft, intense lover Bo remembers. Maybe he was a figment of Bo's imagination. Not that he has the energy to have an imagination right now.

When he meets Sasha's eyes across the locker room, he knows they're on the same page. He still double-checks once they're driving home, because if there's one thing that doesn't belong in a relationship, it's assumptions.

"So, David—"

Sasha shakes his head. "Is worse. Worst. Whatever."

"Yeah." They ride in silence for a few minutes. "I wasn't imagining that, though? For, like, a nanosecond, he was actually like a human being again. And then he went extra hockey dictator on us."

"*Da.*" Sasha nods. "So…"

Bo stretches his legs out in front of him and groans at the pull on muscles aching even after Jordan's best efforts in the trainers room. "So I think we need to go for a repeat performance. Like a friends with benefits thing. Basically what we usually do, just with more sex. If you're cool with that."

Sasha snorts, glancing over as they come to a stop at a red light. "Is rough. Sex very hot. I suffer much for friendship."

"Yeah, yeah," Bo says, rolling his eyes and trying to find a position that doesn't ache. "So yeah. Friends with benefits. If that asshole doesn't kill us first. I don't know if I'll even be able to have sex again at this rate."

"Poor baby," Sasha coos, fluttering his eyelashes ridiculously. "I kiss better?"

"God, you're such an asshole," Bo groans. "Why am I even dating you again?"

Sasha smirks and returns his attention to the road as the light turns green and traffic starts moving again. "I'm best at sex."

It takes literally biting his tongue, but somehow Bo manage not to reply to that—mostly because any disagreement would have been lies, and they both know it.

Silence fills the truck for the rest of the drive, only broken when they're turning into their apartment complex.

"Think David hard to convince?"

Bo grins. "You know me, babe. I like a challenge."

IN THE END, Bo opts for the direct approach.

As usual, David is the last one in the showers after the game, making his captainly rounds of the room and taking a minute with everyone. At least he's not all the way back in super-dick mode yet; none of the rookies are finding excuses not to meet his eye. But his shoulders are tight, his jaw tense. Bo gives Sasha a nod and lingers in his stall, taking his sweet time stripping off his gear and hanging it to be cleaned. He waits until David starts peeling off his own gear before wrapping a towel around his waist and slipping into the showers, nodding at Elvis and Rosie as they head out and leave him alone.

He gives himself a quick, cursory scrub down, parking himself squarely in the middle of the room in stark violation of all observed shower etiquette. It's worth it for the quick flash of surprise across David's face when he comes in, the way he hesitates before sliding under the spray next to Bo.

Even the short time he'd spent waiting gave Bo

the chance to consider and discard several opening lines. In the end, though, as much as he likes seeing David respond to his words, he decides to stick with actions. At least to start with.

"Mac—Bo—" David stutters, startled as Bo crowds into his personal space.

"I want to kiss you," Bo says. Oh, well. Words are kind of his thing. "Unless you don't want me to."

David's eyes dart wildly between his eyes, his mouth, and over his shoulder to the door from the locker room. "I—that's not—we shouldn't—"

"Sash is watching the door," Bo soothes, sliding his arms up David's back and pulling him in until they're pressed together, warm, wet skin to skin. "Do you want me to?"

He waits, somewhat patiently, for the seconds it takes David's resolve to break. For David to close the last few inches between them and devour his mouth like it's been weeks or months, not days since the last time they did this.

By the time they break apart, they're both gasping for air. Bo has no idea when he started moving his hips, dragging his hard, aching cock against the groove of David's hip, but it's not going to take much more of that to make him come.

"We can't," David breathes, his hand flexing around the back of Bo's neck. "Not here."

"Then come home with us," Bo says, forcing himself to move back enough to separate their bodies. He regrets it almost immediately, not just for the cooler air against his skin and the lack of stimulation on his cock, but also for the uncertainty in David's eyes.

David shakes his head. "I—we shouldn't."

"Why the fuck not?" Bo demands. Possibly not his best attempt at tact, but he's doing pretty goddamn good for a guy with at least eighty percent of his blood supply in his cock. "Seriously."

"Why—?" David shakes his head. "So many fucking reasons. We're not in fucking Cozumel anymore, Bo. We have a job to do, and that job isn't to have crazy monkey sex."

Bo rolls his eyes. "You're a hell of a lot better at that job when you're having crazy monkey sex, though. C'mon, David. You don't pick up, you don't date. We're not hurting anybody."

"Oh, so this is a pity fuck?"

David starts to pull away, but jolts to a stop when Bo drags him back in, wraps a hand around both of their cocks. It's a little too dry, water is shit for lube, but it still feels really fucking good. "Does that feel like a pity fuck to you?" he growls, biting down on David's earlobe. "You fucking me while Sash fucked you? That was the hottest shit I've ever seen. Except for everything else we did. This isn't pity. If we were into that kind of shit, we'd be picking up Harty."

He grins when David chokes out a laugh, his hips moving involuntarily to thrust into Bo's grip. "Shut the fuck up."

"Nope. Not 'til you listen. Are you listening?" He punctuates the last word with a little squeeze under the head.

"Y—yeah," David stammers, his whole body shaking.

Bo gentles his grip. "Good. So here's the plan. We're gonna get off, because I don't know about you, but I'm about five minutes from coming, max. Then we're gonna clean up, get dressed, and you're gonna come over to our place and eat whatever Sasha's got planned for dinner. We'll have another crazy-hot threesome, get up in the morning and get off again, then come to practice and kick the Manticores' ass. Sound good?"

"Fuck," David groans, resting his forehead against Bo's. "Yeah, okay."

"Cool." Bo cradles David's face in his free hand,

pulls him in for another kiss, and speeds his hand up. It's more like two minutes before David shudders and comes between them. The hot slickness coating his hand, sliding over his cock, has Bo coming within another couple of strokes, biting down on David's bottom lip before he can stop himself.

They stand there for awhile, leaning on each other and breathing hard, before David straightens with a sigh, turning Bo into the spray and cleaning his stomach with long, wet strokes of his hands.

"We still on?" Bo asks, switching their positions and returning the favor.

"Yeah. If you're sure—"

Bo lays two fingers over David's lips, cutting off the words. "We're sure. I promise."

"Okay." David looks more uncertain than Bo's ever seen him, but he doesn't protest or question further, just helps turn off the showers and follows Bo into the locker room.

Sasha is the only one left, leaning casually against the wall next to the door as they emerge. "Good?" he asks quietly, his grin widening as he takes in the looseness in Bo's muscles, the other thousand and one signs they'd never be able to hide.

"We're good," Bo says breezily, swatting David

lightly on his towel-covered ass before heading to his stall to pull clothes on. "What's for dinner, babe?"

"Grilled chicken," Sasha replies. He doesn't even bother to pretend he isn't watching them dress.

Bo preens a little at the feeling of Sasha's eyes on him, maybe makes a little more of a show of it than he would otherwise. Especially when he notices David watching as well out of the corner of his eye. He bites back a laugh, bends over to pull his underwear up, and mentally fist-pumps when David trips over his own pants.

"Quit show off," Sasha chides gently, shaking his head. "Need David in one piece. For now."

"I don't know if I should be excited or afraid," David says dryly, sitting down to shove his feet into shoes.

Maybe it's the recent orgasm, maybe the prospect of more in the near future, but Bo can't think of another time recently when he's felt this good.

9

SASHA

"Hey," David says quietly from where he's leaning against the bar, watching Sasha work on their dinner.

Sasha doesn't bother looking up from the chicken breast he's seasoning. "*Da?*"

"This—is this okay? Me being here? Cause I can go—"

Now Sasha does look up as he moves to the sink to wash his hands. "Why?"

David stumbles over his words for a second. "I —you guys probably don't get a lot of alone time during the season? And now I'm horning in on it? Seriously, man, say the word and I'm gone."

"No," Sasha says. "Is good. I'm like when you're here."

David drops his eyes to the beer bottle in his hands, biting his lip. "If you're sure—"

"Sure." Sasha does his best to infuse his voice with as much sincerity as he can. "You go, I hear Bo talk about genius plan. All night. Stay. Please."

"Well when you put it like that—" David laughs, lifting his beer for another drink.

"Like what?" Bo asks as he comes out of their bedroom. He crosses the living room and slides his arms around David's waist, snuggling up to his back.

David looks up at Sasha, his eyes uncertain even as he relaxes back into Bo's embrace.

Sasha winks at him before turning to the stove, holding a hand above the grill to test the temperature. "Was tell David he save me from you cuddle all time. Cuddle monster. I need break."

"Oh, I see how it is," Bo says, mock-affronted. He hooks his chin over David's shoulder and pouts in Sasha's direction. "So all the times I wake up with a giant Russian using me as a teddy bear are just a figment of my imagination?"

"*Tochku,*" Sasha agrees. "Got big imagination."

Bo snorts. "I guess David can settle this in the morning."

"Hey," David protests. "When did I become the ref?"

"Unbiased third party," Bo says, letting go of David with one hand to grab his own beer. "Who will side with me, because I'm right."

David makes a rude noise. "First of all, I'm not taking sides here. Secondly, you both cuddled me so much in Cozumel I couldn't even move, so I think that's probably a tie."

Sasha laughs, picking up the chicken breasts and setting them on the grill.

"But you are staying till the morning!" Bo says triumphantly. He meets Sasha's eyes and mouths "best plans," smirking like the competitive jackass he is.

David rolls his eyes, but he doesn't actually look all that put out. "Do I have a choice?"

Bo kisses his neck. "You always have a choice, baby. But if it's up to us, we want to have you here."

"*Da*," Sasha agrees, glancing over to check how much time is left on the rice cooker. "Save me from cuddle monster."

David pats Bo's hand where it rests on his stomach and takes another sip of his beer. "I dunno, man. It's a sacrifice, but I'll do it for you. Because I care."

"Such good captain," Sasha says solemnly, clinking his beer bottle against David's

When David smiles at him, relaxing into Bo's hold, he has to admit that this actually was one of Bo's better ideas. David laughing and joking with them, his body loose, is a far cry from the tightly-wound hockey-playing robot they've been dealing with for most of the season so far.

"Food almost done," he says, turning back to the stove. "Sit down, I bring."

"I can help," David protests, but Bo is already steering him to the table and nudging him into a chair.

"Sash doesn't like people getting in his way in the kitchen," Bo says, taking his own seat. "Maybe someday, if you suck his cock real good, he'll let you help with dinner. But right now, better do as you're told."

David glances over at Sasha for confirmation, lines going tight around his eyes. "My mama would kill me if she saw me sitting on my ass while there was work to be done in the kitchen."

"Mama not here," Sasha says with a wink. "Get forks if you want?"

"Yeah, I can do that." David gets to his feet,

already looking more at ease with a task to accomplish.

He retrieves forks and knives from the silverware drawer and takes them to the table. Once he has the silverware arranged to his satisfaction, he looks up to see Sasha dishing the rice and vegetables onto the last plate.

"Let me help with the plates so you're not juggling all three," he insists, returning to the counter and taking the two plates Sasha indicates.

It's a little strange to only have his plate and his beer to carry, but not bad, Sasha decides as he follows David to the table. Not that he's going to give Bo any more reason to gloat about his genius plan.

"So what's the Christmas plan?" Bo asks, cutting his chicken into chunks so he can mix all his food together like the heathen he is.

"Probably the same as last year," David replies. "Dinner at my house in the afternoon for the families, disgusting Christmas-themed drinks while watching *Die Hard* and all the sequels until everybody passes out. Do we have a head count yet for who's staying?"

Sasha shakes his head. "Soon. Monday?"

"Good enough." David cuts off a bite of

chicken. "How are those skating drills for the d-line going?"

Sasha opens his mouth to answer, but then David's phone starts to nearly vibrate off the table.

"Shit, sorry," David says, swiping at the screen. "Uh, I gotta make a call."

"Everything okay?" Bo asks.

David nods. "Yeah, just a reminder. It's my grandparents' anniversary, so I need to call. It'll just take a minute."

It's more like five minutes before David returns to the table, sliding his phone back into his pocket and picking up his fork. "Sorry about that."

"No worry," Sasha says before Bo can. "You set reminder?"

"You know what I'm like during the season," David says with a shrug. "If I don't set a reminder, I'll forget, and then I'll get a text or a call from my mama about how I forgot. After like, the third time that happened, I just put all that shit in my calendar. Anyway, what were you saying about the d-line drills?"

The strange thing, Sasha thinks as he replies, is how normal all this seems. Of course, David has eaten dinner with them before, many times. But even with the undercurrent of sexual tension, the way David bites his lip when his knee bumps Sasha's under the table, the way Bo watches when David tilts his head back to swallow the last of his beer, it all feels—easy.

It's not like there was an empty space in their lives or anything like that. Sasha has never felt like his relationship with Bo was incomplete, not once in the years they've been together. They've been friends with David almost as long as they've been in this relationship; he's always been there. This just feels like—more. Like a logical extension of the way they work together. Like they were always going to come together this way.

Sasha smiles and sips his beer, listens to Bo and David alternate between flirting and talking goalie strategy. This is good. Good for David, and good for them. Even if it did start with one of Bo's harebrained ideas, it's clearly already something more than just sex.

He wonders how long it will take them to figure it out.

FOR ONCE, Sasha wakes up first the next morning, warm and comfortable aside from the insistent demands of his body. Slipping out of the bed is easier said than done, with David lying on his arm and the way Bo somehow managed to hook their ankles together. But he manages eventually, escaping without waking them and padding silently into the bathroom to relieve the uncomfortable pressure on his bladder.

Urgent needs dealt with, he hesitates once he's back inside the bedroom. They have a game today, and just thinking it has gotten his brain whirring to the point where he doesn't feel very good about his chances for falling back asleep if he returns to the bed. But Bo and David both look so comfortable and the desire to slide back into his empty space, to snuggle up to David's back and savor the warmth and comfort of being with them, is too strong to ignore.

So he does just that, holding his breath as he moves under the covers. David just sighs a little when Sasha drapes a careful arm over his waist, moving unconsciously into the touch even though his breathing stays slow and even. Bo doesn't even stir, his face slack with sleep under the tumbled rat's nest of his hair.

Just as he suspected, Sasha can't quite manage to

fall back asleep, but it's nice, lying there with his eyes closed as the early morning light brightens on the other side of the curtains. Listening to Bo and David breathe next to him, the little noises and rustles as they shift, puts him in a kind of floaty, meditative state. It takes a minute for him to react when David's movements become more purposeful, when Bo makes the little grumbling noise he always does as he's waking up.

He blinks his eyes open just in time to watch appreciatively as David heads for the bathroom; one of the major benefits of the current situation is that he gets to ogle his captain's ass without making anyone uncomfortable.

Bo clearly feels the same, letting out a wolf whistle. "Work it, baby!" he calls, his voice still rusty with sleep.

David flips him off as he disappears into the bathroom, one corner of his mouth curled up in a fond smirk.

"Good morning," Bo murmurs, sliding across the bed and into Sasha's space, pressing a kiss to his jaw. "Sleep well?"

"*Da.*" Sasha tilts his head down, capturing Bo's mouth with his. They trade slow morning kisses, soft and lazy, until the sound of the toilet flushing and the bathroom door opening announce David's return.

"Starting without me?"

The words are joking but there's an edge of uncertainty in David's voice. He's not really looking at them as he stands at the side of the bed, something in the set of his shoulders making Sasha's chest ache.

"*Nyet*," Sasha says easily, sliding free of Bo's grip to pull David onto the bed. "We wait. Just kiss. Now can start."

"I—oof!" The air leaves David's lungs in a startled whoosh as Sasha rolls them over until David is on his back looking up at him, eyes wide and startled.

Bo laughs from next to them, curling up on his side next to David. "What'd I tell you? He's a sneaky motherfucker."

"Is okay?" Sasha asks, cradling David's face in his hands and smoothing a thumb over his cheekbone. "Too much?"

"Nah, it's good," David replies. "What's the plan?"

Sasha shrugs, settling between his legs and letting their cocks brush together. "No plan. Feels good, do it."

David licks his lips, rolling his hips up almost absently. "So if I said I wanted to fuck you?"

"*Da,*" Sasha says instantly, laughing a little at the surprise David can't quite hide. "You think I say no?"

"Sash loves getting fucked," Bo supplies, grinning like it's Christmas and his birthday all in one. "It's his favorite."

Sasha rolls his eyes. "I like all."

"Yeah you do," Bo agrees easily, rolling to the side to grab the lube and dig a condom out of the drawer. "And now I get to watch. This is gonna be great."

"Are you sure—" David asks, his voice hesitant as he takes the lube.

Sasha nods. "Most sure. How you want me?"

He only hesitates a minute longer, searching Sasha's face, but he must find whatever he's looking for, because he slaps Sasha lightly on the ass. "Hands and knees, Ivanov."

"*Da,* Captain," Sasha murmurs, ducking down for a quick kiss before moving off to the side, bracing himself on his hands and knees. "Like this?"

"Perfect," David murmurs, sliding a hand down Sasha's back and stroking it over the curve of his ass. He looks over at Bo. "You ever do this?"

Bo shrugs, stretching luxuriously. "Sometimes. Like I said, it's his favorite. We switch off."

"Any tips?" David asks. His tone is joking, but when Sasha looks back over his shoulder, his face is intent as he drizzles lube over his fingers.

"Start slow," Bo suggests, sliding a hand idly up and down his chest and stomach, not reaching for his cock yet. "Once he's warmed up you can get rougher, but if you go slow enough at first, sometimes you can get him to beg."

"Two against one no fair," Sasha grumbles.

David chuckles, one hand squeezing his hip. "Aww, let me make it up to you."

Before Sasha can figure out a good comeback, David's hands are spreading him wide, one slick finger gliding over his entrance. He does his best to breathe into it, to remember how to relax, letting his head fall down between his arms.

"That's it, babe," Bo murmurs, reaching up to push his hair out of his face and leaning in for a kiss. It starts soft but quickly turns filthy, Bo licking into his mouth like he's starving for Sasha's taste.

Sasha breaks the kiss with a gasp when David finally presses a fingertip inside. It's been awhile since the last time he did this, and he'd forgotten how much it was, how all his attention narrowed down to that one small point of sensation.

"Breathe, Sashenka," Bo says. His long fingers stroke over Sasha's jaw, soft and soothing. "Here, kiss me again."

Kissing helps. Helps keep him grounded in his whole body, not so focused on where David is pumping a slick finger in and out. He doesn't even notice the click of the lube, only realizes that David is adding another finger when he feels the stretch.

"Okay?" David asks when Sasha groans, stopping where he is. His free hand is back on Sasha's hip, thumb rubbing comforting circles on the skin.

"*Da,*" Sasha says. His voice surprises him, breathy and needy. "Is good."

Bo lays a hand over David's on his hip for a minute, starting up that ache in Sasha's chest again. "You're doing so good, babe. Isn't he?"

"Yeah," David agrees, working his fingers in as far as they can go, slow and relentless. "You feel so good, Sasha."

"He's gonna feel ever better when you get inside him," Bo says, trailing a hand over Sasha's stomach. "Can't wait to watch David fuck you, Sashenka. It's so hot, watching him open you up. You look so good."

Sasha bites his lip, the sting distracting him from the electricity running down his spine. David's touch and Bo's words tangle together, lighting him up from the inside out. He's almost pathetically grateful no one is touching his cock right now, because he can't imagine it taking more than a stroke or two to make him come.

"Damn," David says wonderingly. "You really like that, huh?"

"He really does." Any other time, Bo answering for him would be annoying, but now Sasha's just grateful he doesn't have to try and find the words. "I swear sometimes I could talk him into coming, not even touch him."

The hand on Sasha's hip squeezes, then disappears, the lube clicking behind him. "We might have to try that sometime."

"It's a date." Bo leans in, pressing his mouth to Sasha's shoulder. "Three's probably plenty, unless you're just enjoying yourself there."

"Who wouldn't be?" David scissors the two fingers inside of Sasha apart a couple of times before coming back with a third. "But we can move this along, I guess."

Bo laughs. "Such a sacrifice, Cap. Always thinking of others."

"Shut up and hand me the condom," David says mildly.

"Aye, aye," Bo snarks, but he does as he's told.

A shiver races up Sasha's spine as David pulls his fingers free. He doesn't have long to wait, even though it seems like an empty, aching eternity before he feels the blunt pressure of David's cock pressing inside him.

"Fuck," Sasha groans, doing his best not to tense up all over again.

"That's it, baby," Bo murmurs, rubbing soothing circles on his back. "You look so good right now, you don't even know. Tell him."

Sasha's thoughts are splintering in a thousand directions; he can't pull them back together enough to figure out who or what Bo wants him to tell.

"Feel so good," David says, his voice tight and breathless as he pushes in further. "Fuck, Sash—"

"Right?" Bo kisses him softly. "Always so good, baby. You need a minute?"

Sasha shakes his head once the words form meaning in his head. "*Nyet. Khorosho.*"

"Keep going."

"I got that," David says, but his tone is fond, amused, not irritated. "Thank fuck. Don't know if I could stop if I had to."

Bo smiles. "You two look so good together. Okay if I get in on this?"

"I guess?" David's tone is absent as his hipbones press against the curve of Sasha's ass. He pauses there for a minute, buried deep inside him, then starts a slow, deliberate withdrawal.

"Hey, baby. Think you can grab onto the headboard for me?" Bo coaxes, his hands roaming over Sasha's body.

Sasha blinks slowly. Eventually he lifts a hand, curls it over the top bar of their headboard.

"That's it, good job. Now the other one."

Once he's braced with both hands on the headboard, Bo moves in front of him him, worming between his arms for a long, filthy kiss, the soft strokes of his tongue a counterpoint to David's relentless thrusts. All too soon, though, Bo starts kissing his way down Sasha's jaw, his neck. His chest.

"Holy shit," David groans, snapping his hips and driving back inside him.

It takes Sasha a moment longer to realize what's about to happen. "Can't," he groans, unable to string together anything like a complete thought. "I come."

"Then come, baby," Bo murmurs, kissing just

below Sasha's navel. "You know you like getting fucked after. Think David could fuck you till you come again?"

"Fuck me," David mutters. "Seriously?"

Bo grins wickedly up at Sasha. "Let's show him, huh?"

Of course, Bo can't do anything simply, and in the small part of his brain that remains coherent, Sasha can't imagine how he thought he would. Bo amuses himself for a few moments, licking Sasha's cock until every inch of skin is slick and wet, dipping his head to suck Sasha's balls delicately into his mouth.

He waits until Sasha is swearing incoherently, Russian and Quebecois and English profanities mixing together, before finally, finally, closing his mouth over the head of Sasha's cock. He doesn't move much, but he doesn't have to—David's every thrust pushes Sasha's cock into his mouth.

Sasha is too far gone to warn him with words, but by now Bo probably knows the signs of Sasha's impending orgasm better than he does. His only response to Sasha reaching down for a warning tug on his hair is to press closer, humming softly.

The soft vibrations on his cock tip Sasha over the edge, his whole body going tight with the force of his orgasm. It takes a few seconds before he can even realize that David hasn't stopped, fucking him through it without a pause, big hands tight and hard on Sasha's hips.

"Fuck," Sasha gasps, more air than sound.

"Need me to stop?" David asks, hesitating.

Bo pulls off with a wet, obscene sound. "No, keep going. He likes it. I can't usually hold out after he comes."

"I almost didn't," David admits, his voice tight and strained. "I'm close."

"Hear that, baby?" Bo murmurs, pressing up close to Sasha's chest. "You almost made David come. Gonna let him fuck you till he gets there?"

Sasha nods, letting his forehead drop onto Bo's shoulder. He's oversensitive, always is just after coming, but he loves it, the edge of almost too much. There's something comforting about being sandwiched between the two of them, David hard and unyielding inside of him, Bo rubbing up against him, thrusting his cock against Sasha's hip.

In the end, they come almost at the same time. David's steady thrusts get faster and harder, frantic, before he thrusts deep and goes still, his body shuddering against Sasha's. A few seconds later Bo comes wet and messy all over Sasha, fingers digging into his biceps.

"What?" Bo asks when Sasha starts laughing quietly to himself .

"Came same time," Sasha says, his voice choked with laughter. "Thought only happened in porn."

Bo pushes away from him, falling back against the pillows. "Fuck you, Ivanov."

Sasha laughs harder. "Just did. Need minute."

"No more," David decrees as he slowly pulls out. "We have a game tonight."

"Listen to captain," Sasha says solemnly. "Very important."

Bo sighs, rolling his eyes so hard that Sasha is surprised they don't actually fall out. "I literally signed up for this."

"*Da,*" Sasha agrees cheerfully, rolling off the bed and stretching, savoring the slight twinges. "Come. Shower."

Their shower wasn't exactly designed for three professional hockey players, but they make it work.

"HEARD ANYTHING ELSE ABOUT MICHAELSON?"

Bo asks over breakfast, crunching his bacon obnoxiously.

David shrugs, mixing nuts into his oatmeal. "Still on IR. He's getting better, but it's slow. Six weeks minimum for the arm. Plus concussions are a bitch."

"Truth," Sasha agrees, cutting off a bite of omelet. "Petrov say doctors think he recover."

"Russian hockey mafia strikes again." Bo bumps his knee against Sasha's under the table. Judging by David's little grin, he probably does the same on the other side. "Think they'll trade him?"

They all frown at that. Nobody likes to think about it, but it happens, and Michaelson has missed a good third of the games this season.

"Abs have plenty of cap space," David says finally, but the little vertical wrinkle between his eyebrows doesn't go away. "They'd be dumb to trade him if there's a chance he can get back up to speed."

"Stupid things all time in hockey," Sasha points out. "Petrov worried."

Bo sighs. "Nothing we can do about it."

They finish the rest of their breakfasts in silence, gathering their things to head to the arena for practice. It should be strange, having David there for their pre-practice routine on a game day, but it doesn't. It feels good, solid. Like the way things are meant to be. The way they move around each other in the apartment, getting ready, the wrangling over music on the drive—it's good.

"We're the best friends with benefits ever," Bo crows softly in his ear when David peels off at the arena to talk to Coach White about something, and it's all Sasha can do not to roll his eyes.

"*Da,*" he says instead, patting Bo gently on the head. "Best plans."

10

DAVID

"Coming over tonight?" Bo asks, plopping down in the stall next to David's.

David hesitates, glancing around the room. It's almost empty; most of the team has already left to drown their sorrows. The few who remain aren't really talking, the mood subdued after their embarrassing loss to the Krakens. "I should make the rounds, buy some drinks. I should buy you a drink."

"I don't fucking know why," Bo mutters, picking at the knee of his pants. "Five to fucking one. Some goalie I am"

"Hey," David says softly, wrapping a hand around the back of Bo's neck and squeezing gently. "That's not on you. You can't block every fucking puck. They had over sixty shots on goal. You stopped all but five. That's fucking incredible, Bo."

He huffs out a bitter laugh. "If you say so."

"Okay, that's it," David says, pushing to his feet. "You're coming with me, and we're gonna go have a drink with the rest of the team. You're gonna let us tell you you did a good job and you're not gonna argue. Got it?"

"What's in it for me?" Bo asks sullenly.

David glances around, leans in even though no one's close enough to hear him. "If you behave yourself, I'll take you home after and blow you."

Bo licks his lips and swallows hard, his face flushing. David can't help the small surge of pride at the sight. It's harder than he expected to step back, not to pull Bo close in front of everyone. But he can't, he reminds himself. That's not what this is.

Sasha appears next to them, buttoning his shirt and tucking it into his slacks, his hair still damp from the shower. "Ready!" he announces, smirking a little when he notices the expression on Bo's face.

"Let's go," David says quickly. He's pretty sure Sasha won't ask what he'd said. Not in the middle of the locker room. But that edge of uncertainty is enough to get him moving.

"*Da*," Sasha agrees, slinging an arm around each

of them. They can't fit through the door like that, of course, but as soon as they're in the back halls of the arena he pulls them in again. "Drinks?"

David forces himself not to lean into the touch too much, but it's hard not to. On the other side, Bo has no such compunction, snuggling into Sasha's side. But that's different, David reminds himself. "Yeah, drinks. Gotta treat our goalie right."

"Best goalie," Sasha agrees, squeezing Bo a little closer.

Bo opens his mouth, catches David's eye, and closes it again.

"What you do?" Sasha asks, grinning at David. "How you get him shut up? Must teach me trick."

They have to separate again to leave the arena, the security guard on duty nodding at them as they head out the door, clearly seeing nothing out of the ordinary in three hockey players walking so close together. There's no one else nearby once they're outside, though, so David shrugs and says "I promised him a blow job if he behaved."

"Oh!" Sasha smirks. "Good plan. Why I not think of this?"

"Why didn't *I* think of this?" Bo retorts. "I could've been getting bribery blow jobs for literally years."

David can't help but laugh. "Seriously, neither of you thought of this before? How come the single guy is the only one to come up with this?"

Bo opens his mouth to speak as they reach the truck, then frowns when David keeps walking. "You're not riding with us?"

"If I leave my car in the lot again they're gonna start thinking it's abandoned," he says. "Don't worry, I'll meet you there."

He doesn't pause long enough for them to argue, just keeps walking. It's probably stupid to insist on taking two vehicles when he's almost certainly going to spend the night at their place. Again. But he needs the separation to remind himself of what he's know from the beginning.

This isn't going to last.

If he was smart, he thinks as he backs out of his parking spot, he'd cut it off now. Quick and clean, no more waiting to see how long it takes before they get tired of having him around. But they're so close to a playoff spot, even with the loss tonight. He can practically taste it; they all can, even if none of them are willing to say it out loud, to jinx it.

He's only got so much willpower. And they keep inviting him over, or worse, just assuming he'll be there. They keep touching him, kissing him, fucking him, and it would take a stronger man than David to say no to that. They weren't wrong before, about him being too tense. But now, even with the final push for the playoffs, he's a whole lot less stressed than he was earlier in the season. Some nights they're too tired and sore from practice or games to fuck, but just sitting with them on the couch for some dumb Netflix show, Bo's head in his lap, is—it feels good.

It's not fucking with them, it's not fucking with the team, so David just needs to stop worrying so much and just enjoy it while it lasts. Time enough to figure out his dumb feelings in the offseason.

They're waiting for him when he gets out of his car, pulling him inside JP's before he has time for any further introspection. He buys a drink for Bo— and so do Elvis and Dino, a silent apology for the quality of their defense. Sasha buys a drink for Singer, to celebrate the only goal of the night. The mood in the room is less sullen than the locker room, more determined. If they win on Saturday against the Banshees, or if the Abs lose their next game—they can all do the math.

"Don't stay out too late," David says, pushing to his feet after finishing his beer.

"Yes, Mom," Harty says, his voice as nasal and

obnoxious as he can make it, which is a lot.

David flips him off as he heads for the door, incredibly aware of Bo and Sasha behind him. It's hard to believe it doesn't look suspicious to anyone, the three of them leaving at once. But no one comments. Either they assume it's some captain thing, or they're so used to thinking of Sasha and Bo as a unit that it doesn't occur to them that David could be involved as well.

Bo slings an arm around his neck as soon as they're outside, effectively pulling him out of the downward spiral of his thoughts. "Well?"

"Well what?" David asks.

"Did I behave?"

David can't help but roll his eyes at the ridiculous sight of a grown-ass man, a professional hockey goalie, batting his eyelashes like he's trying to signal passing planes. "Let's put it to the Russian judge. What do you think, Sash?"

"Was pretty good," Sasha allows with a grin. "Think he deserve reward."

"Fuck yeah I do," Bo crows, squeezing David closer and tossing Sasha his keys. "Home, James."

It's Sasha's turn to roll his eyes. "Come on," he sighs, peeling Bo off of David. "We see you there?"

"I'm right behind you," David confirms.

DAVID BARELY GETS the door of their apartment closed behind him before Bo pounces, pushing him back against it. "I think somebody promised me a reward?"

"Did somebody say that?" David teases, his hands falling automatically to Bo's hips. "I don't remember that."

"Sash, David's being mean." Bo turns to pout over his shoulder toward where Sasha is sprawled in the corner of the couch.

David takes advantage of his inattention to start them moving in that direction. "C'mon. You're drunk, you should sit down."

"I had three beers," Bo protests, but he lets himself be moved. "And Sash drank most of the last one. I'm not drunk. I'm barely even buzzed."

"Still, you small," Sasha puts in with a lazy grin. "Might be drunk. Need tuck in bed, sleep off."

Bo flips him off, flopping down onto the opposite corner of the couch. "You guys are the worst. Why do I like you again?"

David grins, sinking to his knees. "Because we're good in bed?"

"If you say so," Bo huffs.

He subsides when David's hands land on his knees, stroking slowly up his thighs and back down again. "How about I remind you?" David asks softly, keeping his touch light and teasing.

"Yeah, okay."

"I don't know if that counts as enthusiastic consent," David muses, glancing over at Sasha. "What do you think, Sash?"

Sasha pretends to frown in thought, even though he can't keep the corners of his mouth from tipping up. "Not seem that enthusiastic to me. Maybe he too tired?"

"Seriously, fuck both of you," Bo grumbles, letting his head fall back against the couch. "I swear to God, I'll just jerk myself off right here."

"Rude," David laughs, finally reaching for his waistband, undoing the button and carefully pulling the zipper down. "You don't want me to blow you here while Sasha watches? So he can tell me what you like?"

Bo shivers at the words, his cock twitching inside his boxer briefs. "Fuck," he says weakly.

"Is that a yes?" David teases, pulling his underwear carefully down and letting his cock spring free, hard and flushed red, a drop of precome already beading at the tip. "Cause I can stop, if you're not into this."

"Seriously, fuck you," Bo says, reaching out to curl a hand around the back of David's neck. "Do you want me to beg?"

David lets himself be pulled in for a kiss, deep and wet and filthy. "Maybe another time."

"Then I think you promised me a reward and I'm tired of waiting—"

Bo cuts off with a sharp inhale when David leans down and licks over the head of his cock. Sasha shifts next to them, clothing rustling, and when David looks over, he's curling a hand around his cock where it juts out of his unbuttoned slacks, giving it one long, slow stroke.

"What do you think?" David asks him, staying close enough that his breath blows warm over Bo's cock. "Should I tease him some more?"

"Maybe little more," Sasha rumbles, his eyes hot on them. "He like a little tease."

Bo groans when David licks again, little kitten licks down his shaft. "Fuck you, no I don't."

"You sure seem into it," David teases, but he's getting a little impatient himself. He allows himself one long, lingering stroke of his tongue back up before closing his mouth over the head.

"Fuck, yes," Bo groans. He lets his hands fall down to the cushion next to his hips, thighs trembling under David's hands. "Shit, that's so good."

David devotes himself to the task at hand. He'd forgotten how absorbing it was to do this, the hot, solid weight of a cock on his tongue, the salty-bitter taste, the powerful feeling of finding what makes Bo react. A flick of the tongue just under the head makes him swear, his hands clenching on the couch cushions. The barest scrape of teeth makes his whole body jolt up, thrusting into David's mouth and almost choking him before he manages to relax his throat and take it.

"Look so good," Sasha murmurs, stroking his free hand down David's arm. "Hot."

"One of these days—" Bo gasps, shuddering, when David swirls his tongue around and takes him deeper. "One of these days I wanna watch you two. Sash always gets to watch. I want a turn."

David hums, just for the chance to watch Bo's reaction, to feel it run through his body.

"Can do that," Sasha agrees, his voice tight. "What you want see?"

"Fuck, so many—shit, so many things." Bo moans a little, stroking a hand over David's head. "Fuck, David, I'm close."

He pulls off reluctantly, replacing his mouth with his hand. "You wanna watch me ride Sash, maybe? Your own private porno?"

Bo's eyes flutter shut as he thrusts up into David's hands, his whole body tensing as he comes, wet and messy all over David's fist. He strokes him through it, watching his face to figure out when it tips over into too much.

"Fuck," Bo sighs, slumping back against the couch.

"Good enough reward?" David asks, leaning in for a kiss.

Bo hums softly into the kiss, clinging a little before pulling back. "Pretty good, yeah. Ten out of ten, would go again."

Sasha laughs, his free hand curling around David's arm and pulling him closer. "Looked good from here."

"Yeah?" David lets himself be moved, enjoying the little thrill from how easily Sasha can move him around. "Enjoy the show?"

"*Da,*" Sasha agrees, lifting David's semen-covered hand to his mouth, licking a broad stripe up his palm. "Was hot."

"Shit," Bo groans. "You're killing me. I cannot get hard again this fast. I physically can't."

David shivers, unable to tear his eyes away as Sasha slowly, methodically, cleans every last trace of semen off his hand. When the palm is clean, Sasha sucks one finger at a time into his mouth until David swears he can feel the hot, wet suction on his cock, hard and aching where it presses against his slacks.

"What you want?" Sasha asks, letting the last finger slip free of his lips with a wet, obscene sound.

"Honestly, it's not going to take much," David admits, pressing the heel of his hand against his cock. "A stiff breeze might make me come at this point."

Sasha grins wickedly, unbuttoning and unzipping his slacks. David sighs with relief as the pressure against his cock eases, then sucks in his breath again when Sasha shoves his underwear down and pulls him into his lap.

"This stiff enough?" Sasha asks, getting one big hand around both of their cocks.

David groans, wanting to believe it's from the pun, but the sudden sensation is almost overwhelming. Sasha's cock is hot and hard against his, slick with lube that he hadn't noticed Sasha applying, just enough to make the slide slick and easy. He closes his eyes and thrusts into Sasha's grip, chasing his orgasm.

"Talk about my own personal porno," Bo breathes, stroking a hand down David's back. "Come on, sweetheart. Wanna see you come for us."

The words are more than David can take, tipping him into orgasm before he can catch his breath. Sasha strokes him through it, going still with his own orgasm just as David opens his eyes again.

They sit there for a moment, frozen in a silence only broken by the sound of their breathing. David keeps waiting for it to be weird, to feel strange about the fact that he's having sex with his two best friends. Especially now, sitting on the couch where he's spent so much of his free time over the last several years. It should feel strange, probably.

But in this moment, all David feels are the conflicting but equally strong desires for a shower and to fall into a soft bed. So whatever. Plenty of time to think about that in the offseason.

"I kinda just want to go to sleep right here," Bo says, wriggling a little deeper into the couch cushion.

"Jordan will straight-up kill you if you fuck up

your neck sleeping on the couch," David replies automatically, like he hadn't just been thinking basically the same thing. "Come on. Shower, then bed."

Bo sighs dramatically. "So bossy. Between you and Sash I'm never gonna get a minute's peace."

Sasha grins, pulling David in for a kiss before letting him up. "Such trouble, need two men keep you in line."

"Chirp, chirp, chirp." Bo shakes his head and allows David to pull him to his feet. "It's a good thing the sex is awesome."

"*Da*," Sasha agrees, following them down the hall. "Best sex."

David lets himself be undressed and pulled into the giant shower stall with them, somehow ends up washing Bo's hair as Sasha scrubs his back, and does his best just to be in the present moment. To enjoy it for what it is.

It's enough.

DAVID TAPS on the office door, waiting until Joelle calls "Come in!" to push it open.

"Coach said you wanted to see me?"

She smiles, gesturing him to the chair across

from her desk. "Nothing bad, I promise. We're just going through the team and checking with people who haven't updated their emergency medical contacts in awhile. It looks like you haven't changed yours since you signed with us."

He has to stop and think for a second, but that sounds right. "Yeah? I mean, we can just leave it with my parents. Not like they're gonna be able to get here very quickly from L.A. if something happens, but they'd probably appreciate hearing it from one of you guys instead of SportsCenter."

"Okay, we can do that if you want." She pulls a file out of a teetering stack, somehow managing without sending an avalanche to the floor, and makes a note on a piece of paper inside. "We do like to encourage our athletes to have someone local serve as their medical power of attorney, in case immediate decisions have to be made. It doesn't have to be a family member or significant other, it could be a close friend?"

"I'll think about it," David says shortly, pushing to his feet and trying to keep his tone even. "Was there anything else?"

Joelle shakes her head. "No, that's all. I'll stop taking up your valuable time. Good luck against the Gargoyles tonight!"

"Thanks," he mutters, escaping as fast as he can without actually running toward the weight room to get some cardio in before heading home.

"Everything okay?" Bo asks when David steps on the treadmill next to his. He's taking an easy jog, not even out of breath. Which is good for the team, but means he has no problem talking. Not that Bo would ever let something minor like lung capacity stop him from talking.

David shrugs, setting the program and hitting the start button. "Nothing big. They just want me to have somebody local for my medical power of attorney, since my parents are so far away. In case."

"Ah."

They jog in silence for a few moments, their feet falling into the same rhythm without David noticing at first, and then it's all he can hear. He knows it doesn't mean anything, really, but it's hard for his stupid brain not to read significance into it.

"You could put us down," Bo finally says, breaking the silence. "Me and Sash. We're here, and if anything happens in a game we'll probably be on the ice, too. Get Joelle to stop politely nagging you so you can focus on captaining."

"I—" David can't think of a good reason to say no. He doesn't want to say no, really, and that's the problem. It's everything he wants, for all the wrong reasons. But it's a good idea. Whether they're fucking or not, as much as it hurts to think about the inevitable future time when they're not fucking, Sasha and Bo are his best friends. "Yeah, okay. If you don't mind."

Bo shrugs, dropping down to a walk as the treadmill hits the cooldown phase. "I'll check with Sasha, but I can't think of a reason he'd say no. Fuck, it'd probably be a good idea for you to be on ours, too. In case something happened with both of us at once."

David focuses on keeping his breathing steady and even. Casual. "Yeah, okay. Let me know and I'll do the paperwork. Joelle will be happy, anyway."

"Yup," Bo agrees, lifting the hem of his t-shirt up to wipe sweat off his face. "Always a good thing."

A good thing, David repeats to himself. *This is a good thing. A sensible thing.*

If he keeps repeating it long enough, he might even believe it.

"Oh shit," he says out loud as the realization hits him.

Bo raises his eyebrows in question.

"I'm gonna have to explain this to my mama."

11

BO

"I'm gonna find David a boyfriend," Bo announces on one of their increasingly rare solo drives to the arena. Usually David just rides with them; it's dumb to take two vehicles if they're all going to and from the same place, but today he had to stop at his house for something or whatever. So it's just the two of them.

Sasha glances over at him, eyebrows raised. "Thought we being boyfriends?"

"No, a real boyfriend," Bo replies. "Not that this friends with benefits fake boyfriends thing isn't fucking awesome. And not just the sex. But you know David. Eventually he's gonna want a real relationship. I'm just gonna help him find a good guy."

Sasha opens his mouth, then hesitates for a

second before speaking. "You think that work? Think David be okay?"

Bo shrugs. "Why wouldn't he be? If you can't trust your best friends and occasional fuckbuddies to pick out your future boyfriend, who can you trust?"

Sasha sighs, the one that means *I think you're being silly but I'm not going to argue about it*. Which is a whole lot better than the one that means *I'm going to guilt you until you change your mind*. Bo hates that one.

"It'll be okay," Bo reassures him, patting him gently on the arm. "Remember how we agreed I make the best plans?"

"I not remember agree to that," Sasha deadpans, his eyes crinkled at the corners.

Bo grins back. This is going to be perfect.

HEY, what do you think about hockey, Bo texts his college roommate. Honestly, he can't figure out why he didn't think about Andre for David before. He's laid-back enough not to get rattled when David gets super intense, has a dry, wicked sense of humor, and he's super easy on the eyes. Or he was the last time

Bo saw him. It's been a couple of years, but a guy who spent that much time on his hair probably isn't gonna let himself go.

This is perfect. He feels a little uneasy, but that's probably just because there's no predicting how David and Andre will hit it off. Even though they're kind of perfect for each other on paper. This is a genius plan.

Still dumber than baseball, is the response he gets after a couple of hours. *why?*

talk to me when baseball catchers have to wear my pads, Bo shoots back, rolling his eyes and grinning. *I have this friend, he's a player, exactly your type*

Andre's response is almost instantaneous. *Nope. No can do*

what? Why?

first of all, I swore off athletes. got tired of being body-shamed if I want to eat pizza or have a cookie

Bo frowns. *David's not like that. unless you ask him to help*

Look, I'm sure he's a nice guy, Andre sends back, and even after all this time Bo can practically see him rolling his eyes even without the emoji. *but my fiance's not into sharing, so I'm gonna have to pass*

!!!!!!!! Bo frowns at his screen. *Dude, how did I miss this?*

He gets three laughing emojis in response. *At this point in the season I swear a bomb could go off on Twitter and you wouldn't notice. and you're never on insta.*

Well congrats, even if your deal isn't super awesome and open like mine

not all of us want to fuck every rando that crosses our path, Andre retorts. *different strokes, man. good luck setting up your 'friend'*

The quotes around the word throw him for a minute, but Bo decides it's better not to ask. *Fine, be that way. send me an invite one you set a date, k?*

You got it. Say hi to your Russian bear boyfriend, you walking stereotype

Bo sends him a string of middle finger emojis before locking his phone with a sigh.

"Okay?" Sasha asks. Across from him, David mirrors his concerned expression.

"Yeah, it's cool," Bo says, digging into his chicken and pasta with a sigh. "Andre's getting married, apparently. I didn't even know he was seeing someone, but I guess it's serious."

David's forehead furrows as he flips through his mental roster. "Andre?"

Bo flaps a hand dismissively. "My roommate from college, the whole two years I finished before I got called up. Nice guy, used to play baseball. I don't remember if you met him last time he came to visit or not."

"I don't think so," David says, his face clearing once the mystery is explained.

Sasha gives Bo a meaningful look as David returns his attention to dinner, but Bo just shakes his head. Andre would've been great, but Bo didn't get to be a CHL goalie by giving up at the first obstacle in his path.

Operation Get David a Boyfriend is still a go.

Bo nudges Sasha with an elbow. "What about that guy?"

It takes a second, but Sasha follows his gaze to the guy leaning against the bar. "Too pretty," Sasha says dismissively.

"I resemble that remark," Bo says, mock-offended. "Pretty people can be nice, too. Right, Xander?"

"Huh?" Xander doesn't even bother turning away from Jordan. "Yeah, sure."

Bo sighs dramatically. "Jordan, would you please tell your boyfriend to stop making eyes at you for two seconds so we can have a conversation?"

"Nah, I'm good," Jordan says with a grin, ducking his head a little the way he still does when someone calls Xander his boyfriend.

"Ugh, get a room," David chirps, sliding back into the booth and passing out beers.

Jordan and Xander don't even bother flipping him off. "That sounds like a great idea," Xander says, sliding out of the booth and pulling Jordan with him. "We'll see y'all tomorrow."

"'Y'all?'" Bo repeats, raising his eyebrows. "Jordan, you're rubbing off on him!"

"Every chance we get," Xander says with a wink, ignoring the groans from the rest of the table. "Night, you three. Don't stay up too late; we have another game tomorrow."

Shortly after they disappear out the door, Bo's phone buzzes in his pocket. When he pulls it out, there's a text from Xander. *that guy at the bar is Jamie. Nice guy, but he wants to go out like, every night, and stay out way too late. Not really compatible.*

good to know, Bo sends back. It's a relief, because the last thing he wants to do is set David up with somebody who's not going to work out.

After a couple of minutes, though, curiosity gets

the better of him. *Don't you want to know why I was wondering?*

"Home?" Sasha murmurs in his ear. And yeah, that sounds like a plan.

Later that night after he, David, and Sasha have cleaned up and crawled into bed and he finally checks his phone, he sees a new text from Xander. *none of my business. Until you break our captain*

have a little faith, he sends back

"Who're you texting?" David mumbles, his eyes mostly closed. On the other side of him, Sasha is already snoring softly, the noise only slightly muffled by the pillow he face-planted in.

"Just Xander," Bo murmurs. "Go to sleep."

David sighs, wriggling a little before settling into the mattress. "'Kay. You too."

"Okay," Bo agrees. Setting his phone aside, he allows himself to be pulled into nestle against David's side. "Good night."

"Night." David breathes, his voice barely audible in the darkened room.

No, Bo thinks to himself as he drifts off. That guy wouldn't have worked for David at all. He'll just have to keep looking.

"…AND when you're ready, make your way to a seated position on your mat," the yoga instructor says, her voice low and soothing.

Bo stays in savasana for a few more seconds before rolling to his side and pushing his way up to sit. Despite the aches and pains of the last few weeks, the tension of their playoff spot being so close and yet not quite there, he feels great. He always feels great after yoga, invigorated. Like his skin should be glowing with the sense of well-being. Sure, the flexibility is great, but that feeling is the thing that keeps him coming back.

The instructor waits until everyone is seated before pressing her palms together at her heart and bowing over them. "Namaste."

"Namaste," the class choruses softly in response.

Bo always feels vaguely like a tool saying it, but more like a tool when he doesn't. Given the choice, he usually chooses to err on the side of lesser tool-ness. But today he's not thinking much about it, mouthing the word on autopilot. He's been a man on a mission ever since he caught the cute guy two mats over checking him out. Not for him; between Sasha and David, there's an excellent amount of sex in his life. But Cute Guy looks like excellent boyfriend material for David.

There's no rush, though. Not when he feels like this, warm and loose and right. He bides his time, rolling up his mat slowly and evenly. It's nice to notice that Cute Guy does too, waiting for the people between them to clear out before moving over and clearing his throat quietly.

"Hi," he says, smiling. Somehow he strikes a balance between shy and confident and it's pretty damn endearing. "I'm Braden. I was wondering if you maybe wanted to go get coffee?"

Bo smiles back, because coffee is great. It will absolutely be easier to feel out cute dude at coffee than standing here with the instructor starting to look impatient that they aren't getting out already. He's just about to say yes, when it happens.

"I know this great vegan place around the corner? Their soy lattes are amazing, and they have the best vegan scones in the city."

It's a challenge to control his expression, but Bo has a lifetime of practice speaking to the media, so he manages. Barely. "Man, I wish I could, but I have to get to work."

"Oh. Okay."

"Good class," Bo says cheerfully, doing his best to shift the energy from flirty to just bros. "Maybe I'll see you next time."

He can practically see Cute Guy reclassifying him as "probably a meat-eater" as he backs slowly away. "Yeah, maybe."

It's a shame, Bo thinks, as he finishes gathering his things and heads for the door. But seriously, life is too short to date a vegan.

The mental image of Braden staring at one of their heavy-protein meals in horror is pretty funny, though. He's still amused by the time he makes it home.

"I DON'T GET IT," Bo complains. He's pretty sure Sasha isn't listening to him, but that's okay. The road to the airport is tricky at the best of times; it's probably best that Sasha pays attention to the road. He mostly just needs to talk it out anyway. "There are a ton of hot guys in this city, and a lot of them are queer. Why am I having so much trouble finding someone for David?"

Sasha shrugs, eyes still firmly on the road. "Maybe trying too hard? Doesn't have to be perfect guy."

"I mean, it kinda does. At this point, if they hit a roadblock, David's gonna nope right out. It's hard enough to keep him in this super casual thing we're doing." He pauses at Sasha's quiet snort. "What?"

"Something else funny," Sasha says dismissively. "Maybe not right time find boyfriend for David. Maybe offseason better."

Bo considers that. "Probably. I just want him to be happy, you know. He takes so much on himself. He needs someone to help with that."

They come to a stop at a red light and Sasha reaches over to squeeze his knee. "I know. It happen eventually, when time right."

"Yeah, you're probably right," Bo agrees with a sigh. "And in the meantime, he's got us. And now we get to have roadie sex!"

"Hotel walls very thin," Sasha cautions, but he's smiling as he puts his hand back on the steering wheel.

Bo smiles too. "I know, I know. But we'll have adjoining rooms. Maybe one of us will be in a corner again."

"Maybe worry about winning games?" Sasha asks, pulling into the parking garage.

The only possible response to that is a rude noise. Bo makes it enthusiastically. "We've prepped for that as much as we can. I'm just trying to keep us from getting wound too tight in the meantime."

"Sure," Sasha agrees blandly as he parks the truck. "So thoughtful. Selfless. Like hero."

"Exactly," Bo agrees, climbing out and grabbing his bag from the back seat before slamming the door behind him.

Conveniently, David pulls in a couple of spots down from them while Sasha's getting his own bag out. "Ready to kick some Banshee ass?" David asks, closing his door and walking over to where they're waiting for him.

"Abso-fucking-lutely," Bo replies, his voice maybe a little on the manic side. Just a smidge. Well, possibly more than a smidge, given the epic side-eye he's getting from both David and Sasha.

"What's got you so chipper?" David asks. "Did Sash let you get extra espresso shots again? I thought we talked about this."

Bo shakes his head. "Nah, I'm just excited. We get to have roadie sex!"

Watching David's expression war between turned-on anticipation and responsible team captain is maybe the most fun Bo's had all week.

12

SASHA

It takes Sasha the entire roadie to put his finger on the problem. On the surface, everything is good. Sure, they lose to the Reapers, but it's in OT so they still get a point, and they beat the Banshees soundly, 4-2. The team is doing well for this point in the season, only a couple of guys out on injured reserve. Sure, they're all nursing something—Xander's shoulder, Harty's knee, Sasha's ankle. David's taping his wrist pretty much all the time, and even though the doctor swears Bo's fingers are just sprained, not broken, they're playing Ricky and LK a lot more to give him time to heal.

But honestly, all of that is par for the course at this point in the season, and they're doing a lot better than some other teams. The Abs only just got Michaelson back on the ice in a no-contact jersey and the Chimeras actually had to play their emergency backup goalie for like seven minutes in their last game.

So things are going well, really. They're two wins away from clinching a playoff spot, and Sasha knows he's not the only one who can practically taste it. They're still having fantastic, mind-blowingly hot sex with David. On paper, everything is great. But something, specifically something with David, is off.

He's on the plane back to Milwaukee when he realizes. Probably the worst place ever for an emotional revelation, but nothing about emotions has ever been convenient. And Sasha, unlike Bo, can actually keep things to himself at times. So he settles back in his seat, turning it over in his head in case he's wrong.

By the time the plane touches down, though, he's pretty sure he's right. Now the question is, what to do about it.

"Come over tonight," Bo half-asks, half-tells David when the rest of the team has peeled off to their respective vehicles and it's just the three of them.

David hesitates. "I haven't been in my house for more than five minutes in like, two weeks," he jokes, not meeting their eyes. "I should probably go say hi, so it doesn't get lonely."

"We can go to yours then," Bo agrees, so happily oblivious that Sasha kind of wants to shake him. "We haven't fucked in your bed yet! Sash, why haven't we fucked at David's yet?"

"Maybe David want be alone," Sasha points out, as gently as possible.

Bo turns to David, his forehead furrowed. "Oh, sorry. Look, I don't always get things—Sash can tell you. It's cool if you want to be alone. You can just say so. I know I'm, like, a lot."

"No," David says quickly, reaching out to squeeze Bo's shoulder. "No, that's—I just—You guys can come to mine. If you want. I'd like that."

"Sweet!" Bo's face clears and he practically skips toward their truck. "What are we waiting for?"

SASHA WAITS FOR HIS MOMENT. It's surprisingly hard to find a time to talk to Bo when David isn't around. He shouldn't be surprised, probably. Out of the three of them, he thinks—he knows—that he's the one paying the most attention to this thing between them, to how much more tightly they're entwined in each other's lives. But even he hadn't fully realized how little time they spend apart.

He finally gets his chance when David has an appointment for x-rays and then MRIs of his wrist; they'd offered to go with him, but he waved them off. It's not like they could sit in the room while he gets x-rayed, he points out. And they can wait just as easily and a lot more comfortably at his place.

"Something up with David," Sasha starts while Bo flips aimlessly through channels, because if there's one thing he's learned in this relationship it's that there's no point beating around the bush. Blunt is best when it comes to getting concepts across.

"Huh?" Bo sets the remote down and turns more toward him. "Like what? He's been a lot better lately, I thought. Since Cozumel."

Sasha nods, because that's true. David is more laid back now, less likely to go into hockey captain robot mode and forget that the team needs things like sleep and food and rest. But that's not what he's talking about. "Not that. He—" he hesitates, trying to find the right words in English. "He—keeps self apart? We always ask, always invite. He say yes, but doesn't ask."

Bo bites at his lower lip. "Huh. No, he—no, you're right. How did I not notice this?"

"Too busy fucking," Sasha teases. "Think with little head, not big head."

"Hey," Bo says, but it's half-hearted. "So. What are we gonna do about this?"

Sasha shrugs. "Is why I talk to you. Should say something?"

"I don't know," Bo says slowly. "It might work. Or it might really fuck things up. And we're two wins from the playoffs."

"Bad time," Sasha agrees.

They sit in silence for a few moments.

"Hey, Sash?"

When he looks up, Bo's lip is red and swollen where he's been chewing on it. "*Da?*"

"I think—I don't want David to get a boyfriend."

"No?" Sasha knows he probably shouldn't be stringing his boyfriend along like this. It's not nice. But he's had to deal with months of Bo's genius plans. He can't help it. "Thought you said would find one for him? Perfect one?"

Bo frowns even more. "I don't want him to have a boyfriend. Especially not a perfect one, if one exists, which I doubt. I want him to be our boyfriend. Like, what we're doing. But permanent."

"Congratulations," Sasha says dryly, probably enjoying the confusion on Bo's face more than he should. "You last one to know."

"Fuck off," Bo says automatically. "What?"

Sasha shrugs. "Basically already boyfriends? Have sex, spend all time together. Boyfriends."

"Yeah, but—" Bo cuts off, blinking rapidly. "Holy shit, have we been dating him this entire time?"

"Finally," Sasha sighs, maybe a touch overdramatic, but not enough to justify the pillow Bo tosses at his face. "Hey!"

Bo sniffs. "Serves you right for not telling me."

"You not listen," Sasha points out, not entirely unreasonably, he thinks. "Too excited about genius plan."

"Yeah, but, like, it's your job to tell me when I'm being a dumbass."

Sasha throws the pillow back, gently. "When I sign up for this?"

"Comes with the package, baby," Bo teases, grinning softly. "You knew what I was like before this started."

"Is true," Sasha admits.

Bo sighs. "So. What now?"

"Should probably wait until end of season," Sasha says slowly. "Give time, in case it fuck things up."

"Probably," Bo agrees, sighing again. After a minute, he brightens. "But we can court the shit out of him in the meanwhile."

Sasha blinks. He's normally able to follow Bo's train of thought, but this is one of the rare exceptions. "What?"

"Really step up the boyfriending." Bo continues, his enthusiasm unabated. "Make him hate the idea of not being with us. Yeah, this is going to work."

"Like last genius plan?" Sasha asks, because he can't not take an opening like that.

Bo just grins, completely unfazed. "Better. You watch."

Sasha shakes his head. "Maybe David not want boyfriend. Boyfriends."

"O ye of little faith," Bo retorted. "If he didn't, he would've cut this off already. No, we just have to make sure he realizes."

And honestly, that's a decent point, as much as Sasha wants to keep needling him. "Fine," he sighs.

Just because Bo has a point doesn't mean he's always right. You just have to look at the "find David a boyfriend" plan to see that, although Sasha laughed so hard after the near-miss vegan story that he almost thought he'd pulled a muscle.

"You'll see," Bo says. "Trust me."

Sasha captures his face in his hands, pulls him in for a kiss. "Always."

HE KEEPS WAITING for Bo to put his plan into effect, but things stay pretty normal after David comes back from his tests. It's an off night and they've already done practice and as much working out as they're allowed at this point in the season. So they laze around his house, bickering amiably over what to watch on David's monstrous TV and savoring the near-boredom. David even ices his wrist without complaint.

Once it's a little later in the day, Sasha makes dinner in David's frankly ridiculous kitchen, thick steaks that he sears on the grill before popping them in the oven to finish, mashed potatoes with brown butter and heavy cream. Carol has been making worried faces about all of their weights even though she's been the team nutritionist for nearly a decade, knows better than a lot of people how the later part of the season starts whittling them down to the bone. So he sprinkles cheese and crumbled bacon over the top of the potatoes and considers making cookies later.

Bo and David both make appreciative noises over the food, devouring it with the single-minded focus of professional athletes. Once they're done and pleasantly stuffed, dishes cleared away, they collapse back onto the couch in a soft, satisfied daze.

It's all very domestic. Sasha knows they've been doing this exact thing for over a month, but somehow it feels weightier now. More intentional. Maybe the fact that he and Bo both acknowledged that they want this permanently, seriously. Either way, Sasha finds himself picturing a string of evenings just like this one, halfway to a food coma, watching Bo and David heckle the SportsCenter announcers before they switch the channel to a cooking show.

"Nooo," Bo groans when a contestant forgets the eggs in their cake.

"At least they make cake," Sasha says mildly,

enjoying the indignant expression he gets in return. "When you make cake? Never."

Bo huffs. "Excuse you, I've made a cake before. And I didn't forget the eggs, either."

"I call your mama, she say you lying?" Sasha gestures vaguely in the direction of his phone. He has no intention of getting up to get it, but Bo doesn't need to know that.

"Just because you were born knowing how to cook doesn't mean other people can't do it, too," Bo says stubbornly. "Besides, half the fun of these shows is yelling at the contestants when they fuck something up. Or sympathizing. If they're not a bag of dicks."

David nods solemnly, his eyes drooping. "It's true. Nobody wants to root for a bag of dicks. And everybody needs somebody to yell at."

"That's deep, man," Bo says, leaning on David's shoulder. "Is that why all the fans have a love-hate relationship with DuPuy? Because they like yelling at him?"

"He nice guy off ice," Sasha points out. "Only bag of dicks when play him."

Bo snorts. "That's fucking plenty, thanks. At least we don't have to play the Banshees again."

They sit there for a moment, the unspoken fact

that they might have to face the Banshees in the playoffs hanging heavy in the air. None of them mentions it, though, even though they're clearly all thinking it.

On the TV screen, a cake topples to the floor in slow motion, jolting them out of thoughts of the season. "Fuck," David breathes. "What's he gonna do now?"

They watch cooking shows until the second time David jerks awake with a start when he dozes off, his head tipping onto Sasha's arm.

"Bed," Sasha says firmly, nudging them both up off the couch. "I get lights. Go."

Probably the strangest thing about moving through David's house, checking the locks and turning off the lights, is how strange it isn't. He's been here before, of course; they both have. But this simple intimacy makes something tighten in his chest, another vision of a future he didn't realize how much he wanted.

By the time he makes it into the bedroom, they're both nestled into the big bed, curled up together with a space left for him. He turns off that light, too, moving across the darkened room to the bathroom and rushing through his bedtime routine.

He slips under the covers and wraps himself

around David's back, getting a sleepy mumble of greeting in return and then a chorus of soft snores. His last thought before he drifts off to sleep is to hope that, for once, Bo's genius plan works.

I want this.

13

DAVID

David is focusing on hockey. That's what he's doing. Hockey, and the last three points standing between them and a playoff spot. His team needs him to be completely, absolutely focused. They deserve that, from their captain, and that's what he's going to give them.

Focus.

He's not thinking about the fact that this—thing with Sasha and Bo just keeps happening. That they spend almost all of their nights together, either at his place or at theirs. That the sex, if possible, keeps getting hotter. That it's getting harder to imagine a time when it won't be like this.

Hockey.

Three more points.

That's what matters.

Not his inevitable broken heart.

"YOURS OR OURS?" Bo asks, probably too loud, but David's having trouble caring. The rest of the team is varying stages of tipsy or drunk around them, celebrating a shutout against the Chupacabras. Their playoff spot is so close they can fucking taste it, all of them more drunk on the possibility than the alcohol.

So what does it matter if Bo's too loud? If the team hasn't figured it out, and David's not so sure that they haven't—Xander keeps giving him smug looks—they will eventually. Eventually this is all going to crash and burn and he'll be left to pick up the pieces. But if this is all he gets, he's going to enjoy it while it lasts. Enjoy the fact that they've stopped asking him if he's going to come over and just moved straight to logistics.

"Yours is closer," he says, running a hand through Bo's hair. "But you pick. You got a fucking shutout!"

"Hell yeah!" Bo agrees. He leans into David's touch, his eyes sliding shut.

Something in David's chest clenches, aches. It's too much, it's so close to what he wants, and he only gets to have it for a little while. He pulls his hand away under the guise of reaching for his beer and does his best to ignore the frown on Bo's face.

"So?" he asks once Sasha slides back in the booth. "Goalie's choice. Where are we going?"

"Yours," Bo finally says. "We're out of breakfast food at ours, but I'm pretty sure Sash has some bacon stashed in your fridge."

Sasha shrugs. "You tell me where we be, I make sure we have food there. Not leave good food to rot."

"Fair," David agrees. He's suddenly itching to get out of there, to a place where they're not observed, where they can just be. Where they can drive all these thoughts and anxieties out of his head. "Ready?"

"Yeah, if I drink any more, I'm just gonna pass out." Bo stretches his arms up over his head, his untucked shirt riding up with the movement.

David's seen him naked, it's ridiculous for that little flash of abs to have his mouth going dry. But everything about him right now is ridiculous; this is a small thing to dwell on. "Then let's get you home, Sleeping Beauty."

As soon as the words leave his mouth, he realizes what he'd said. But he can't take them back, shouldn't draw more attention to the fact that he thinks of his place as Bo's home. The only way out is through. He slides out of the booth, not meeting either of their eyes, and pulls his coat on.

"*Da,*" Sasha agrees, getting to his feet and pulling Bo out of the booth. "Morning skate soon. Need sleep."

"Eventually," Bo says, so quietly it's almost inaudible over the noise of conversation, but the smirk is still clear in his voice. "Sleep eventually."

David can't help smiling back, not sure if he's relieved or disappointed that neither of them picked up on his implication. "Well, yeah. Shutouts deserve a reward."

"Sweet," Bo says as he leads the way out to the parking lot. "I love rewards."

Somehow they'd all ended up piling into David's car for the ride from the arena to JP's, but when they find it in the parking lot, Sasha clears his throat. "Maybe I drive?" he suggests. "You in back, start reward on way?"

"Ohhhh," Bo breathes, his eyes wide and dark in the dim glow of the streetlights. "Yeah, I like this idea."

"You think so now," David retorts, crowding him up against the side of the car for a kiss. He feels reckless, unstoppable. Anyone from the team could walk out and see them right now, and he doesn't care. "We'll see how you feel after I spend the whole drive teasing you."

Bo sucks in a long, shuddering breath, his cock visibly half-hard in his slacks. "Jesus. Get in the fucking car already."

David hits the unlock button and hands Sasha his keys. "After you."

"Fuck me," Bo mutters, sliding into the back seat.

"Not yet," David replies. He follows, moving over into the middle seat, into Bo's space. "Better get your seatbelt on. Safety first."

Bo's hands are shaking so hard that it takes him three tries to get his seatbelt buckled, and David can't help the surge of power that rushes through him at the sight as he closes the door behind him and buckles his own belt. "Good boy," he murmurs when Bo finally succeeds, sliding a hand through Bo's hair again.

"Ready?"Sasha asks, meeting David's eyes in the rearview mirror as he adjusts it.

"We're good," David answers, holding Sasha's

eyes as he fists his hand in Bo's hair and tugs slightly. "Right, Bo?"

Another tug just as Bo opens his mouth and whatever he was going to say trails off in a soft whimper. It's a little awkward to reach over with the seatbelt restraining him, but it's worth it to turn Bo's face toward him with his free hand, to pull him in for the barest brush of lips.

Bo tries to press in closer, to deepen the kiss, but between his seatbelt and David's hand in his hair, he can't move very far. David kisses him softly, teasing him with infinitesimally deepening pressure, slight flicks of his tongue to contrast with the steady pressure on his hair.

"Please?" Bo gasps, swallowing hard as his eyes flutter closed. "God, please—"

"Please what?" David asks, doing his best to keep his tone casual. "What do you want, baby?"

Bo doesn't seem to notice the endearment that slipped in, too desperate for sensation. "Touch me, please."

"I am touching you," David replies, pretending he can't feel Sasha's too-knowing eyes on him. "You don't like this? This isn't good?"

"More. Please." Bo bites at his bottom lip,

looking half-wrecked already, just from a few kisses and David's words. "Please, I want—I need—"

David lets the hand cradling his face slide slowly, slowly down his neck, finding all the little hot spots he's discovered since they started this, savoring the feeling of Bo trembling under his touch. He keeps it feather-light, just firm enough not to tickle, as he dips his fingertips under Bo's collar. "Like this? Is this what you want?"

Bo swallows, the sound almost a sob. "More, God. David, please—"

He nearly chokes on his words when David lets his hand move lower, flattening the no-longer-crisp fabric of his shirt and rubbing a thumb over his nipple. "That?" he asks doing it again just to hear the noise Bo makes. "You want more of that?"

All it takes is a glance down to see that Bo is fully hard now, straining against the fabric of his slacks in a way that looks almost painful. "Please," he breathes again, like it's the only word he remembers, the only thing he can say. "Please, please…"

"You're not gonna come in my car," David tells him, only barely managing to keep his voice steady. "Understand?"

"Yes, yes, please—" Bo does sob when David

drops a hand to his cock, squeezing through the fabric.

David gives him one slow stroke before letting go and reaching for the zipper on his slacks. "We're about halfway to my place. I'm going to tease you until we get there, but you aren't going to come, are you?"

"Oh God," Bo moans, a long, shaky exhale as David pulls down his zipper, his eager cock springing free through the opening as the pressure on it is relieved, the fabric of his boxer briefs damp where the head presses against it.

"You didn't answer me," David says mildly, tugging lightly on Bo's hair. "Are you going to come in my car?"

Bo pulls in a shuddering breath through his nose, his voice barely audible when he finally does speak. "No."

David tugs again, still gentle, just enough to light up his nerve endings. "No, what?"

"No I'm not gonna come in your car," Bo says, the words tumbling out in a rush.

"Good boy," David says again, and this time it gets him a full-body shudder. "So I'm going to tease you until we get there, and Sasha's going to pull into the garage and close the door. Do you know why?"

Bo shakes his head, his hips shifting against the seat as David tugs the elastic of his boxer briefs down, freeing his cock.

"Because," David says, the plan taking shape in his head as he says the words. He's never done anything like this before, never had the nerve. Maybe this will be the thing that pushes them away, but he wants this, with a deep, aching need. Wants it enough to take the chance. "You're gonna walk in the house just like this, with your cock out."

As soon as the words leave his mouth, he wishes he could take them back. Bo's eyes go wide, flying to his face, and David doesn't dare glance over to meet Sasha's eyes in the mirror.

"Then what?" Bo asks, his voice shaky, after what feels like an eternity.

"You'll walk to the bedroom like that," David says, when he's sure his voice will sound somewhat normal. "Then you're going to take off your clothes, get on the bed, and suck me off while Sasha fucks you. And when he's done, I'm going to fuck you."

Bo's eyes slide closed again and his whole body seems to melt into the seat. The only visible tension left in is body is in his cock, which twitches visibly at David's words. "Yeah. Please."

David has to kiss him again, has to tilt his head to the right angle to lick inside and devour his mouth. His free hand keeps moving, stroking over every inch of Bo's body he can reach except his neglected cock. When he has to come up for air, he takes a long, deep breath, and moves over to lick around the shell of his ear.

Every touch is purposely too-gentle, not enough, from the way David nips lightly at his earlobe to the skim of a palm over his nipple, pressing just enough to be felt, a barely-there tease. He loses himself in it, the way Bo's body arches into his touch like he's wordlessly begging for more, the little whimpering breaths that slip out of his mouth, the thick smell of sex that fills the air.

He's so absorbed in his self-appointed task that he only realizes they've arrived when he hears the click as Sasha presses the garage remote button. Lifting his head, he keeps one hand firmly in Bo's hair, skimming the other one down his thigh.

"We're here," he murmurs, squeezing Bo's knee before letting go. "Are you ready?"

Bo blinks his eyes open. "I, uh. Yeah. Yeah, I'm ready."

Sasha brings the car to a stop and hits the remote again before turning the engine off. They wait in silence while the garage door closes slowly behind them, then Bo reaches for his seatbelt buckle with shaky hands and opens the door.

When David finally brings himself to meet Sasha's gaze, he's not sure what he expects to see. Judgement, maybe, or disappointment, or something else negative. Resentment or jealousy. But all there is is heat and something else, something he can't quite identify.

They follow Bo into the house without speaking, the tension between them winding tighter with every step, every movement, until David can hardly breathe with the force of it. It's almost like porn, Bo walking through the darkened house fully dressed in his game day suit except for his cock, hard and bobbing in the air with every step he takes, but no porn David's ever seen has had him flying this high this fast.

As soon as he passes into the bedroom, Bo shrugs out of his suit jacket, tossing it onto the chair that already holds a pile of their discarded clothes. His hands move to his shirt buttons next, slipping them free one after another as he walks toward the bed.

"Is good look on him," Sasha says, as though they're continuing a conversation that had already begun. "Like porn."

Since David just had that exact same thought, he can't disagree. "Yeah, if the whole CHL goalie thing falls through, he could probably make decent money as a stripper."

"Very flexible," Sasha agrees with a grin. "Maybe need install pole in corner for practice?"

"Fuck you guys, I'm standing right here," Bo says, starting to unbutton his shirt cuffs.

Sasha's grin widens, becomes almost wolfish. "Can see that. Should turn around, give us show."

"Fuck you," Bo repeats but he does turn, the unbuttoned sides of his shirt framing his chest and abs as he works the cuff buttons free. "I'm not dancing."

"Nobody asked you to dance," David says mildly. "You already have your instructions."

He can practically see the memory of his words flow through Bo's body, and fuck, that's a heady feeling. Taking this strong man apart, wrecking him with a few words, a few fleeting touches. David has to bite down on his lower lip to stay focused. If he's doing this, if he's calling the shots, he has to pay attention, to take care of Bo. Of both of them.

Bo shrugs out of his shirt, muscles rippling, and lets it fall to the floor. His chest is visibly moving with the force of his breath, his mouth wet and red where he licks his lips, but he takes his time, sliding his hands slowly, deliberately down his chest, over his abs, to find the button on his slacks and work it slowly, teasingly free.

"Good," David says, partly to take back his control, partly to see the way Bo reacts to the praise. "So good. Isn't he, Sash?"

"*Khorosho*. Very good," Sasha agrees, his voice hoarse.

Out of the corner of his eye, David can see him start stripping out of his own suit, fast and efficient. But he can't tear his eyes away from Bo, the way he's pushing his slacks and boxer briefs slowly down his legs, bending at the waist and never breaking eye contact.

"Hell of a show,"David says hoarsely.

"And you didn't have to pay for it," Bo replies with a wink, crawling onto the bed with an exaggerated waggle of his hips. He looks back over his shoulder. "Now I believe somebody was gonna fuck me? And if you want me to suck you off, you might want to get your pants off, at least."

David shakes himself out of his reverie and

starts taking off his clothes while Sasha retrieves the lube and joins Bo on the bed. "Getting bossy again. Sasha, think you can do something about that?"

"Think maybe," Sasha agrees, running his hands down Bo's back in one long stroke, then spreading him wide. "Still little loose. Not take much."

"Oh yeah?" David asks, kicking his socks off and climbing up onto the bed. "Now that's interesting. Too bad we have a game tomorrow. Maybe in the offseason, we could try that. Just slick up and push in, a little at a time. Think you'd like that?"

Bo starts shivering about halfway through his little speech, his hips pushing back into Sasha's hands. "Fuck. Yeah. Maybe."

"So good," David murmurs, brushing his hair back from his forehead as he settles with his back against the headboard. "You ready?"

"Yeah," Bo agrees, nuzzling his face into David's palm. "Yeah, c'mon."

David gets his free hand around his cock, coaxes Bo down—not that it takes much coaxing. Bo takes him almost all the way in with that first hot, wet slide of his mouth. Every instinct he has is screaming at him to thrust, to push up and fuck Bo's mouth hard and fast until he comes. But that's not what they're doing here.

"Don't make me come," he orders, tugging on Bo's hair to emphasize the command. "I don't want to come until I'm inside your ass, understand?"

Bo nods as much as he can and slows his movements to something more sustainable. David looks up—if he watches Bo's mouth, stretched wide around his cock, he's going to come regardless of other considerations—just in time to see Sasha push one slick finger slowly inside him.

It's a strange sort of connection, feeling Bo's reactions vibrate through him from where Sasha's working him open, all the way to where his mouth is wrapped around David. Within a short, measureless time, he's too distracted to really focus on blowing David, shivering and moaning and pushing back, wordlessly begging for more.

"Is he ready?" David asks, meeting Sasha's eyes.

"Think so," Sasha says, petting his free hand absently over the curve of Bo's ass and scissoring his fingers apart. "Want me tease him more?"

David considers it, and then his own stamina and refractory period. "No, go ahead."

Sasha nods, pulling his fingers free. He grabs the lube and slicks up his cock while Bo redoubles his efforts to suck David's brain out through his cock. He doesn't have much time for that, though, before

Sasha is lining himself up and pushing inside with one hard, fast snap of his hips.

Bo cries out, a wordless sound that vibrates down David's cock, his eyes fluttering shut. Sasha doesn't waste any time, wrapping his hands around Bo's waist and setting a fast, almost punishing pace. Every thrust pushes Bo's mouth onto David's cock, which is good, because he doesn't seem to have the focus to do anything but be there, rocked between them with each movement.

By the time Sasha comes, slamming in with one last, hard thrust and holding on tightly as he shudders through his orgasm, David is holding onto control by his fingernails. Every sense is overloaded—the sounds that Bo and Sasha are making, watching them come together, the smell of sex heavy in the air, texture of Bo's hair and skin under his hands, all of it driving him higher.

"My turn," he rasps, pulling Bo's head up and off. "You can come while I'm fucking you, but no touching. If you want to come before I do, you're gonna come on my cock, understand?"

Bo nods, his mouth red and swollen, hanging open as he gasps for air. Sasha pulls out and moves to the side, patting Bo lightly on the ass as he collapses to the bed, his chest heaving.

David almost, almost forgets the condom—no, that's not true. He wants to forget the condom, but that's not okay. He's not Sasha; he and Bo don't have that kind of relationship, and he isn't—can't be —the kind of dick who forces that decision. So he grabs one from the drawer and rolls it on with quick, impatient movements, shaking off the strange feeling of melancholy as he lines himself up and sinks inside.

The physical sensation is so good his eyes almost roll back in his head, hot and tight, but loose enough that he can still push in easily in one stroke. Bo moans under him, pushing back to try and get him even deeper. "Please," he whimpers, dropping down to his elbows, his forehead pressed into the mattress. "David, please."

"I've got you," David promises, getting a grip and starting to move. "You're being so good for us, isn't he, Sash?"

"So good," Sasha agrees, stroking up and down Bo's back. "Always so good."

David frees up a hand and threads it through Bo's hair. "Yeah. Feel so good, hot and tight, all slick with Sash's come. I'm gonna come fucking you, come inside you. Are you gonna come for us? You close?"

"Close," Bo gasps, his back bowing with David's grip on his hair. "God, please, please—fuck, right there—shit, don't stop—"

"I'm not going to stop," David promises, pulling just a little harder on his hair and focusing on keeping the same angle, nailing his prostate mercilessly. "Not going to stop till I come. God, I wish I could fuck you forever, just never leave. Feels so good—"

Bo comes with a soft cry, his body tightening down around David's cock like he's trying to pull David's orgasm out of him. It only takes a couple more thrusts into that tight heat before he's coming, too, lost in the overwhelming sensation.

When he regains awareness of his body he's slumped over Bo's back, his hands braced on the mattress the only thing keeping them from collapsing. He pulls out carefully, removes the condom and ties it off, then stands when he feels like his legs can support him again.

"I'm gonna get a washcloth and some Gatorade," he says softly, "I'll be right back."

"Kay," Bo says, smiling a sweet, fuck-drunk smile at him. "Don't take too long."

David's heart does that clenching thing in his

chest again. It's very inconvenient. "I won't," he promises.

True to his word, he's back in a few minutes. It takes a bit of convincing for Bo to let himself be cleaned, but David gets his way in the end. They all down their Gatorade without complaint—nobody wants a hangover at morning skate—before settling in for the night.

If this is all he gets, David thinks vaguely as he lies there in the dark, with Bo and Sasha wrapped around him, that's fine. He just has to protect himself, control his emotions.

He falls asleep ignoring the voice in his head telling him it's already too late.

14

BO

When Bo wakes up in the morning, it takes him a minute to realize what feels off. He's in David's bed, but that's become normal enough that it shouldn't be bothering him. His muscles are pleasantly sore from last night—he grins at the memory, stretching luxuriously just to feel the twinge and pull—but honestly, the bruise on his thigh from the puck he stopped in the third hurts worse.

He brings his arms down from the stretch, one landing on Sasha's shoulder, the other on empty bed, and there it is. Sure, David could've just gotten up to use the bathroom or something, but the sheets are cold.

Bo sits up, rubbing his eyes where they're still a little gritty.

"Mmm?" Sasha sighs, blinking his eyes open. "You okay?"

"I don't know," Bo says slowly. "David's not here."

Sasha rubs his hands over his face, shoving his hair back. "Bathroom?"

"The sheets are cold," Bo persists, feeling a little silly, like a child insisting that a monster really did eat his parents.

"Maybe he make breakfast," Sasha says, but the furrow between his eyebrows says he's worried too. He sits up and swings his legs over the side of the bed, heading over to grab his boxers from the floor. "We go see."

Bo follows suit, blushing a little when he remembers how his boxer briefs and slacks ended up in a puddle by the side of the bed. "Hey, Sash? All that, last night, were you good with that?"

"Was good with me," Sasha answers instantly, sliding a hand over Bo's shoulder. "You?"

"Uh, yeah, I was totally into it. One hundred percent. Maybe more. Just, you know, checking in. You'd say something if you weren't cool, right?"

Sasha grins, tugging him in for a quick kiss. "*Da*. Promise."

"Okay, good."

"You, too," Sasha insists, taking his hand and lacing their fingers together, his eyes serious. "Promise?"

Bo smiles, following him out of the bedroom. "Cross my heart."

As soon as they open the door, the smell of bacon wafts in from the living area. They follow their noses to the kitchen, where David stands in a pair of sweatpants and a t-shirt, a platter piled high with bacon on the island. He's turned away from them as they come into view, stirring vegetables in a skillet, but Bo sees his shoulders tense when he hears them.

"Morning," Bo says, because "fake it till you make it" might as well be tattooed across his chest. "Smells amazing. You didn't have to cook for us."

David shrugs, his eyes still firmly on the food. "I felt like it. Sasha's been cooking for us so much lately."

"I not mind," Sasha says mildly, brushing a gentle hand over David's back as he crosses to the coffeepot. "Not complain about this, either."

"Omelets'll be done in like ten," David says,

shooting a sideways glance at Bo, there and gone again. "Coffee's ready, though."

For lack of anything else to do, Bo heads over to the coffeepot, mimicking Sasha's light touch on his way. Once he has his coffee poured and doctored the way he likes—for once, without anyone chirping him about his flavored creamer—he settles in near the stove, watching David stir the onions and peppers in the skillet. "You okay?"

"Feel like I should be asking you that," David mutters, with another one of those quick, darting glances. "Last night—"

"Was fucking awesome," Bo interrupts. "Unless you didn't enjoy yourself?"

David's eyes snap to his. "Uh, I think It's pretty clear I did. But—I should've asked? Before starting something like that?"

"Maybe," Bo allows. "But it was hot as fuck."

"*Da*," Sasha agrees. "Such hot."

David ducks his head, but he's grinning as he stirs the vegetables. "Don't front, Ivanov, I know your English is better than that."

"Maybe," Sasha says, hiding his own grin in his coffee cup. "Still hot."

"Yeah," David agrees, looking back up at Bo,

something achingly vulnerable in his eyes. "It was okay? It wasn't too much?"

Bo shakes his head. "It was just enough. My only complaint was that you didn't come in me, instead of the condom."

If he hadn't been watching very closely, he wouldn't have seen the little shiver that danced down David's spine at that, the naked want on his face for just a second.

"Actually," he says, as casually as he can manage. "We should do that. You got tested at the beginning of the season, right?"

David turns toward the bowl of beaten eggs waiting on the counter, his throat working as he swallows. "Yeah. Same time we all did."

"Sweet." Bo takes another drink of his coffee. "And you haven't hooked up with anyone else this season."

"You sure?" David asks, looking up at him with challengingly raised eyebrows. "You're not with me all the time."

Bo snorts. "Pretty fucking close, these days. Not at the start of the season, though. Did you?"

"No," David admits. He pours the egg mixture into the skillet, shifting the veggies around so it can cover the whole surface. "No time."

"So then, we're good," Bo says firmly. "You're clean, we're clean. None of us has been with anyone else since the last time we were tested. Next time you can skip the condom."

Sasha clears his throat. "Unless you want condom."

"Right. That."

David pushes the cooked omelet back from the edges of the pan, tilting it to let the still runny mixture flow into the empty spaces. "I—no, I'm good with that."

"Good. And you should totally do that ordering me around thing again." Bo pretends to swoon a little, fans himself with his hand. It's worth it just for the look David shoots him, simultaneously fond and exasperated. "So fucking hot."

"Yeah, okay," David agrees, reaching for the shredded cheese and sprinkling some on top of the omelet, expertly folding it in half. "You want to throw some bread in the toaster? And there's oatmeal in the rice cooker."

Bo whistles, reaching for the bag of bread and moving over to the toaster. "Damn, you don't fuck around with breakfast, do you?"

"We're all a little underweight," David retorts.

"We need our strength. And to not have Carol fussing over us."

"Is true," Sasha agrees, getting out bowls and spoons and carrying them to the table. "Big game tomorrow."

They work together to get their breakfast on the little table in the breakfast nook. The fact that he and Sasha know where everything is, just as much as in their own apartment, has something warm building in Bo's chest. It's a little thing, but David let them into his space, his home. Maybe, just maybe, they've got a shot at this.

He's so lost in his own thoughts that he doesn't realize David's psyching himself up to something until he blurts out "We don't have to always do it that way."

"Huh?" Bo asks inelegantly, his mouth half full of bacon and oatmeal.

David looks like he kind of wants to dig a hole and never come out, but he soldiers on. "I mean, if you wanted to order me around sometimes—I think I'd like that."

Bo looks at Sasha, sees his own surprise and interest reflected back there, and has to take a moment to tell his cock that now is *most definitely not the time.* "I—that sounds fucking hot, too. If you're sure."

"I—" David shrugs helplessly, his eyes firmly on his plate. "I haven't tried it before. But I think about it, sometimes. When I'm tired of being the captain. I just—I want to not have to think for awhile, sometimes."

"Oh," Bo says softly. "Yeah, I get that. We can do that. And if it doesn't work, you'll say so, right?"

David's jaw sets stubbornly. "I can take it—" he breaks off when Bo punches him lightly in the shoulder. "Ow, Jesus."

"That's not the point, dumbass," Bo tells him. "You don't just keep doing shit if you don't like it, if it's not working for you. Have you been doing that with us? Just suffering in noble silence or some shit? Because I swear to God—"

"No," David interrupts. "No, I haven't—I wouldn't."

Bo subsides. "Well—good. But don't, okay? Even if we never do that, even if we stop in the middle and try something new, the sex will still be fucking amazing. Promise us."

"Promise," he says solemnly, meeting first Bo's eyes, then Sasha's.

"Good," Sasha says with a decisive nod. "Now

eat. Or we get distracted with sex talk and food get cold."

Bo laughs. "Yeah, that'd be a tragedy. Food now. Sex talk later."

"We have morning skate in an hour," David protests, cutting off a bite of his omelet.

"You say that like you think I don't work well under pressure," Bo replies with a wink. "Eat up, you're gonna need your strength."

David groans around the food in his mouth, chewing and swallowing. "I literally signed up for this."

"*Da,*" Sasha agrees unsympathetically. "Both did. Now have someone share with."

Bo just grins and applies himself to his breakfast. He's going to need his strength, too.

HE FINDS himself with a rare quiet moment that afternoon; David is off at an appointment for cryotherapy on his wrist and Sasha is, well, somewhere. Bo isn't worried; Sasha gets like this sometimes, needs to disappear for a few hours. He'll be back.

It's odd, though, being in David's house by

himself. He flips through the channels in David's cable package—nothing—then through Netflix—nothing that looks interesting right now. Switching to Hulu, he puts on an episode of MasterChef Junior, but even Gordon Ramsey being sweet and supportive to adorable kids isn't enough to hold his attention.

Eventually, he gives up, turning off the TV and pulling out his phone. Since no one's here to chirp him, this is an ideal time to use up all his Candy Crush lives. But instead of opening the app, he finds himself tapping on his contacts, then on his mother's name.

"Hi, honey," she says when she answers the phone. "This is a nice surprise. I figured you'd all be doing some kind of team visualization thing or something."

"Nah, that's Tuesday," he says, just to hear her laugh. "How is everybody? How are you?"

He can hear her smile down the line, and it relaxes something in him that he didn't know was tense. "Oh, we're doing fine. Nothing too exciting here, you know how it is."

"I know." He settles back in the corner of the couch, closes his eyes and pictures her in the chair in her home office. "How's Dad?"

"Well, he decided that we need a new backyard fence, but the estimate from the company almost gave him another heart attack, so he's been sulking around the house muttering about scam artists. Oh, and did I tell you that Emma got that scholarship?"

He shakes his head instinctively. "No, you didn't. Mom, you know I said I'd pay for wherever she wants to go."

"Well, I know you did, but you know your sister. She wants to feel like she's contributing."

"Yeah. I can't believe she's graduating this year."

His mother sighs. "You and me both. I wish you could be here."

"Me too, but…" he trails off, not willing to name the reason why he can't commit to it. His mother, after years of this, knows better than to tweak his superstitions, even if he's absolutely positive she's rolling her eyes at him right now.

"Anyway, enough about us," she changes the subject. "Some blogger was saying you broke your wrist. I swear, they write the worst trash. Useless excuses for journalists."

"Wow, Mom, tell me how you really feel," he teases. "Just so you know, privileged insider information and all—I didn't break my wrist."

She snorts. "You think I don't know that? Sasha

would've been texting or calling me as soon as they let him at his phone. He's a nice boy. I was a little worried about you for a while, but you found a good one. When are you going to bring him back for a visit? We want to see you for a little while at least this summer."

Bo hesitates. "I want to see you, too, and so does Sash. We'll have to figure out dates and stuff once we know what the offseason looks like."

"But?" his mother asks.

"Jesus, how do you do that?" he asks, resigned, but not surprised. He's never been able to hide anything from his mom for long, and he doesn't know why he thought he could start now. "I'm literally a thousand miles away."

She laughs. "I didn't stop being your mother just because of some distance. Spit it out, I haven't got all day."

He knows, despite the words, that she actually would wait all day if she needed to, for him to get his thoughts in order. But apparently his subconscious has been working on this, because the words just kind of spill out of him. "I—well, Sasha and I—"

"You're not breaking up!" she interrupts, more a demand than a question.

"No, no, I swear," he hastens to reassure her. "No, but, we—we're seeing someone."

There's silence on the line while she digests that, long enough that he checks the screen to make sure the call hadn't disconnected. "I'm assuming you mean 'seeing' in the romantic sense?" she finally says.

"Uh, yeah." Bo fights the urge to squirm. "It's still new, but I'm—we're serious about this. If we can make it work."

"Well, you never could do anything the easy way," she says, wry amusement in her voice. "And to think, I used to be worried you'd knock some girl up in high school."

It's his turn to laugh. "Not much chance of that, Mom."

"No, I know," she says. "I'm not going to tell you that this might make things harder for you— for all of you. No matter how many times you've gotten hit in the head, you've got enough brains left to know that."

"Yeah," he admits. "But it's—he's worth it."

She takes a deep breath, audible even over the phone. "Okay, then. You'd better bring him with you and Sasha when you come to visit."

"Oh, God," Bo says weakly. "I—he—"

"Don't think you're going to wriggle out of this," she warns. "If he's good enough for you to date, he's good enough for you to bring home to meet your family."

Bo snorts. "Oh, he's good enough. I just wanted a little more time before he saw what kind of crazy people I'm related to."

"Well, time's up," she says mercilessly. "All three of you, this summer, for at least a week. Non-negotiable."

"Maybe I need to start having you do my contract negotiations," he says, only half-joking. "You could make bank as a hockey agent."

She laughs. "No, thank you. Two—well, I guess three, now—professional hockey players is more than enough for me to deal with. Any more and I'd be driven to drink."

"Mom, you already drink," he jokes, trying to pretend he hasn't gone all gooey inside at his mom's casual acceptance that he loves not one, but two men. That the men he loves will be part of her life, part of her family, too.

"I'd be driven to drink more," she says tartly. "And we all know it wouldn't be pretty."

"I don't know, I always think you're pretty," he says, unable to hide the sincerity in his voice.

She sighs. "You should come tell that to my mirror, then."

"It lies," he says confidently. "Wait, how did you know we're dating another player?"

"You barely have time to call your mother," she says with exaggerated patience. "I hardly think you're out picking up on Grindr or whatever the kids are using these days. It was an educated guess. One you just confirmed, by the way."

Behind him, the garage door opens before he has to formulate a response to that. "I better go. Tell Dad and Emma I said hi."

"I will," she promises. "And you have to text me when you tell your dad so I can see his face."

Bo groans. "Maybe I just never come home again."

"I will hunt you down," his mother promises. "Give Sasha my love. And your other man—what was his name?"

"I didn't tell you his name. On purpose. Nice try. I love you."

"I love you, too," she says.

David comes around the end of the couch and settles into the opposite corner, propping his wrist up gingerly on the armrest. Bo waits until he's settled and turning on the TV, then slides across the couch to snuggle into his side, careful not to jostle him too much.

"My mom says hi," he says halfway through the first episode of House Hunters.

"Cool," David says absently, his jaw cracking with a yawn. "Nap?"

Bo smiles, grabbing the throw blanket off the back of the couch and pulling it over them. "Sounds great."

15

SASHA

They have two minutes left in the third and Sasha feels like he may never breathe normally again, even though he's sitting on the bench, has been for almost ten minutes. He and Elvis have skated at least twenty minutes of this game and it's been chippy as hell. He's pretty sure his finger is just sprained, not broken, but it hurts to grip his stick.

They've been tied for what feels like the whole game, the Jacks answering each of the Wendigos goals with one of their own. Bo stops shot after shot, makes impossible save after impossible save, while the forwards do their best to take the game to the Jacks goal. But as the time ticks down toward the end of regulation, the score remains stubbornly tied. Sasha can feel the resignation settling over them, see it in the slump of David's shoulders.

"First line, get out there," Coach White barks when there's a minute and a half left.

Sasha takes a moment to bump David's shoulder with his before he and Elvis go over the boards. A shootout is good, he tells himself with the part of his brain that isn't immersed in hockey. It's fine, they can still get at least one more point—

His self-soothing litany is derailed by shock and awe as he watches David intercept a pass between Gelbart and Hagen, flick it to Xander seconds before the Jacks' defense closes the gap. Xander takes off toward their goal, David and Becks both skating flat out to try and get in good position for a pass. Sasha does his best to block Hagen's path; on his best day, he can't keep up with Xander and David on the ice.

Xander dekes around someone in a gold jersey —someone else goes sprawling at his feet. It's one of those rare moments when Sasha feels like nothing but a spectator, watching as Xander fakes out Reissler, the Jacks's goalie. Watching Reissler go sprawling across the ice, leaving the net wide open, unable to block the gorgeous top-shelf shot Xander hammers in.

The goal horn sounds, David and Becks crash into Xander, driving him back against the boards, and Sasha's there a few seconds later, grinning so hard he can feel his face ache. The buzzer sounds a few seconds later, just as Elvis slams into his back, and that's it. They won. They're going to the playoffs.

"We're going to the fucking playoffs!" Xander screams in his ear, pounding on his and Becks's helmet indiscriminately.

Sasha squeezes an arm tight around David's waist, as much of a hug as he can manage with all of their pads and equipment. The arena is going wild, red and white towels waving, the roar of the crowd finally filtering in now that Sasha doesn't have to retain his laser focus, and the rest of the team pours across the ice to dogpile on them.

Not just the team, he sees, as Jordan worms his way through the crush after a couple of minutes, knocking Xander's helmet off and pulling him down for a frankly filthy kiss. Honestly, though, he deserves it; if Jordan wasn't here, Sasha might have had to kiss him for that gorgeous fucking goal.

And then Bo is there, helmet and mask discarded somewhere along the way, hair sticking up every which way. Sasha can't get free enough to pick him up and whirl him around like he wants to, but with Bo and David both crushed against him, he doesn't mind as much as he expected to.

"Fucking playoffs!" Bo screams, and Sasha nods, all of it still feeling vaguely unreal, dream-like. But he's not asleep—the throbbing in his fingers and his ankle, the shakiness in his legs, the smell of sweaty hockey players, none of that is ever present in his dreams.

This is real. They did it.

"We did it," he says, under his breath, then louder, bubbling up out of him. "We did it!"

"We fucking did it!" David yells back, looking about as stunned as Sasha feels.

They eventually make their way back down the tunnel and into the locker room, less as individuals than as multiple parts of the same raucous, incredulous organism. It's times like this that Sasha can almost feel the connection between the team, the jubilation vibrating through the air, growing as it echoes from one to another and back again.

They're going to the playoffs. Realistically, he knows that it means more, harder work, more exhaustion and pain and strain. There are no guarantees of victory, only the barest chance to try as hard as they can and still maybe fail. But in this moment, none of that matters.

In this moment, there is only joy.

THE CELEBRATION LASTS FOR HOURS, spilling out of the arena to JP's, from JP's to David's house when last call comes and not everyone is ready to go home, to let go of this moment. Eventually though, people take their leave, with lots of backslapping hugs and drunken declarations that they're going to crush the series before somehow managing to climb into a Lyft without breaking anything.

Connolly, Cruz, and Jackson passed out on the couches before they could be persuaded to go home, so Sasha helps nudge them awake and get them into guest rooms, with painkillers and Gatorade waiting next to their beds. Bo pouts when Sasha won't let him take a picture of the way Jackson burrows into Cruz's back in his sleep, but eventually relents.

Sasha stopped drinking around the time they relocated, high off the team energy. And, as much as he hates to admit it, he's too old to drink like the rookies. Even on a night like tonight—or a day like today, he supposes; the first hints of light are starting to hit the horizon—massive hangovers are enough of a deterrent to have him cutting himself off. Besides, someone has to keep an eye on the babies.

He's not sure about Bo or David, not until they meet back in the bedroom. Neither of them is drunk, but they're already tucked into bed, just waiting for him.

"We're totally having celebration sex," Bo mumbles, not opening his eyes from where he's cuddled into David's side. "Tomorrow."

"Today," Sasha corrects. "Already today."

He grumbles. "Fine. But sleep first."

"Sleep," David agrees, his voice nearly inaudible.

It's the last thing Sasha remembers before drifting into sleep.

IN THE MORNING—LATER that day, whatever— there are hungover rookies to feed, press conferences to attend, and a million and one other details to attend. Even if morning skate was cancelled, regular practice wasn't, but the mood on the ice is a more subdued version of last night, excitement radiating off the team so hard it's practically visible.

After practice, Marian makes disapproving noises over David's wrist and orders him to ice it more, declares Sasha's fingers sprained and prescribes the same treatment. She clucks over his ankle, but they all know there's nothing more to be done. Not now.

"Good thing is left hand," he jokes, getting an unamused look in return.

"I don't want to hear about your extracurricular activities, Ivanov," she says, shooing him out of the room. "Get out of here and let me see people who actually need my help."

He tosses her a salute that's only half-joking— she might barely come up to his chest, but she reminds him so strongly of his babushka he half-expects to get rapped on the knuckles with a wooden spoon half the time—and leaves as ordered.

David and Bo straighten up from where they were leaning against the wall as he comes out. "Ready?" Bo asks, heading toward the exit without waiting for a response.

"*Da.*" Sasha shares an amused look with David as they follow in his wake. "Somewhere we need be?"

"We clinched our playoff spot nearly twenty-four hours ago and we still haven't had celebratory sex," Bo replies as soon as they're outside the arena. "That's gotta be some kind of crime."

This time the look he exchanges with David is a lot more heated, the sexual tension settling into place like it never left. "You have plan?" Sasha asks as they get closer to the car.

Bo unlocks it and slides into the driver's seat, not responding at first. Sasha makes the snap decision to join David in the back seat instead of going around to the front. Now might not be the time to start talking about this thing they're doing, but that doesn't mean he can't show David that they want him there. That he's not on the outside in this.

As soon as his seatbelt clicks home, Bo puts the car in reverse and starts backing out. "Yeah, I have a plan. If you guys are up for it. I was thinking about what we talked about before, David. About how sometimes you don't want to call the shots."

Watching the emotions cross David's face is an education—embarrassment, hesitation, but most of all the naked want he can't, or won't, hide. He swallows hard before answering. "Yeah."

"We can do that for you," Bo says, looking up

into the mirror to meet first Sasha's eyes, then David's. "If you want. If you trust us with that."

David takes a deep breath, his nostrils flaring, but his voice is steady when he says. "Yeah. To all of it. I want it. I trust you."

The sexual tension is thick in the air, hanging in the silence until Sasha can't help but break it. "Why we always have these talks in car?" he mock-complains. "Not enough room for good sex. Bad planning."

Bo raises an eyebrow at him. "Or good planning, if you want to start with the foreplay while I drive us home?"

"Ah, I see." Sasha turns to David, reaches out to cup his face, rub a thumb lightly over his lower lip. "This okay?"

"Yeah," David says softly, leaning into the barely-there touch, his eyes challenging. "Hit me with your best shot."

Sasha grins slowly at him, unbuckling his seatbelt and sliding over into the middle seat.

Bo laughs softly from the front. "Oh, you're gonna regret this."

"You think so?" David asks, never looking away from Sasha.

"You thought the thing with the tequila shots

was hot?" Bo asks. "Buddy, you ain't seen nothing yet. Our boy's got some serious moves."

Sasha leans in for a kiss before David can respond. He'd half-considered teasing like David had with Bo the other night, but discarded the idea as soon as it occurred to him. The last thing he wants is for David to feel uncertain. Instead he pushes from the very start, licking inside David's mouth until he can explore every inch of it, sliding his hands under David's t-shirt to find skin.

He can't really push their bodies together like he wants to with the seatbelts holding them back, but that's okay. It's strangely satisfying just to kiss, to let his hands and mouth roam over as much of David as he can reach. He's doing his best to overwhelm David with sensation, but it's a feedback loop, revving him up, too.

It actually takes Sasha a minute to realize that the car is off, not just stopping at a light. He pulls back reluctantly from the hickey he started sucking just under David's jawline when Bo pulls the passenger door open.

"Come on, no fair hogging him," Bo mock-protests, leaning in for a kiss of his own as he reaches across David's body to unbuckle his seatbelt.

It's far from the first time Sasha's seen them kiss,

close up and far away, but something about this moment is different. There's no less desire in the way Bo kisses him, deep and intense, than before. And maybe it's just Sasha's imagination, because he knows how Bo feels, and how he feels, but it seems like there's an extra tenderness in the way Bo's hands cradle David's face as they kiss. The moment when they break apart, but still stay so close, breathing the same air.

It's enough to make him hope that they can make this happen, that they can convince David to be with them for real.

"Okay, let's go," Bo says after sneaking one last kiss. "As someone pointed out, there's not enough room in the back seat for three hockey players to have good sex."

"Not big deal if people stop having foreplay in car," Sasha points out as he slides out behind David, closing the door. "Perfectly good bedrooms everywhere."

Bo grabs David's hand, then Sasha's, and starts towing them toward the apartment door, unlocking it impatiently when they get there and shoving them inside. "Yeah, yeah, less bitching, more walking."

It's probably counterproductive to keep kissing

and touching as they make their way toward the bedroom, but Sasha can't regret it. Not when they slowly strip David along the way, leaving a trail of discarded clothes in their wake. Not when he's moaning into Sasha's mouth as Bo's hands map out every inch of his skin. Not when he already looks wrecked by the time they reach their destination, overwhelmed with sensation, his lips bitten red from trying to hold back his reactions.

"Let us hear you," Bo murmurs, letting his hand slide down to wrap around David's cock, stroking agonizingly slowly. "Come on, sweetheart, we've got you."

David shudders, his eyes sliding closed, and lets Bo nudge him down onto the bed.

"Okay," Bo says, grabbing the lube sitting on the bedside table. "We don't want to put too much strain on your wrist. Do you think you're up for riding Sash? You won't have to move much."

"I—" David blinks slowly, flexes his wrist experimentally but doesn't protest. "I think so."

Bo grins, leans down for a long, lingering kiss. "All right, we'll give it a shot. Sash, go sit up against the headboard."

Sasha obeys, beginning to see the shape of the plan, and definitely on board.

Sure enough, Bo nudges David over into his lap. "Okay, now just relax and let us get you ready, sweetheart."

Relaxation seems to be beyond David at the moment, his whole body practically vibrating with arousal, but he melts into it when Sasha pulls him in for a kiss. Being able to fit together like this, skin to skin, is incredibly satisfying after the extended tease that was their car ride home. Sasha lets himself drift on it for a moment, lost in the sensation.

He's vaguely aware of Bo settling between his legs, so it's not surprising when David jumps a little. "Shhh," Sasha soothes, breaking the kiss but stroking his hands up and down David's back. "Trust us."

Bo takes one of his hands—the right, thankfully, not his sprained left, and drizzles lube over the first two fingers. Sasha knows how to take a hint, rubs teasing circles down between David's cheeks, over and over until David pushes back into the touch.

Pressed together as closely as they are, he can feel David shudder when his finger slips inside to the first knuckle. "*Da,*" he murmurs, keeping his other hand moving over David's skin, pressing a kiss to his neck. "So good."

"Let us make you feel good," Bo says, kissing David's shoulder blade. "You know we can, sweetheart. Just let us."

David shudders again when Bo's hands spread him wide, when Sasha fucks his finger slowly in and out. The noise he makes when Bo lets go of him and comes back with a lube-slick finger, pressing it gently, inexorably inside along Sasha's, is indescribable. He buries his face in Sasha's neck and lets them work him open.

It's one of the most beautiful things Sasha's ever seen. When he meets Bo's eyes, he sees the same feelings shining there.

He almost doesn't want the moment to end, but at the same time, every shift of David's body rubs up against his cock, hard and aching. Sasha waits while Bo adds more lube and another finger, works with him to stretch and prepare David's body, and does his best to ignore the demands of his own.

Finally, finally, Bo pulls his fingers free, kissing David's shoulder again. "Hey, sweetheart, do you think you're ready?"

David nods, his face still pressed into Sasha's neck.

"Can you turn around for us?"

It takes a minute, but David lifts his head and

turns around to face Bo. Sasha waits for Bo's nod before grabbing the lube and slicking his cock up.

"Okay," Bo murmurs, leaning in to kiss David. "We're going to do all the work for you, okay? I just want you to sit back on Sasha's cock for us."

David looks back over his shoulder, shuddering when Sasha lines himself up, then slowly starts to lower himself down. Sasha bites his lip, forcing himself to stay still, not to thrust up and take. They both suck in a breath when the head slips inside, past the ring of muscle.

Sasha lets go of his cock as David sinks lower, stroking up and down his arms as he takes Sasha's cock deeper and deeper, until his back is against Sasha's chest, his ass resting snugly in the cradle of Sasha's hips. Until they're both breathing like there isn't enough air in the room, hard and fast and desperate.

"That's it." Bo moves in closer, kisses first David, then Sasha. "You look so good, you're doing so well. You need a minute?"

David nods, letting his head fall back onto Sasha's shoulder.

"Okay, sweetheart," Bo soothes. "Just let us know when you're ready."

Sasha's pretty overwhelmed with sensation

himself, the tight, hot clutch of David's body around his cock, all the places where they're touching, skin on skin. He thinks he can be excused for not realizing what's happening at first. It takes him a minute to put together the wet, obscene noise he's hearing with the look on Bo's face, the fact that one hand has disappeared from sight.

David starts moving on top of him, distracting him with little filthy grinds, like he's trying to get Sasha in even deeper. "Ready?" Sasha asks, waiting for the nod before he starts to thrust up, just a little at first.

"Fuck, you look so good like that," Bo says, his voice breathless. "Could watch you two forever. But not tonight. Tonight we're going to make you feel good, sweetheart. Is Sasha doing that? He making you feel good?"

One of David's hands comes up to curl around the back of Sasha's neck, holding him close, the other clutching his thigh. He nods, little noises falling from his mouth each time Sasha moves. With the little range of motion he has available, it's more of a grind than a thrust, but it's enough to light up every nerve in his body, and David seems to feel the same.

"Stop for a minute," Bo orders.

It takes Sasha a few seconds for the words to make sense. But eventually the meaning filters through and he stops moving, as much as it goes against every instinct screaming at him.

David makes a protesting noise, his eyes fluttering open to look accusingly at Bo, who moves into his space, kissing him gently.

"I know, I know," he says when he lifts his head. "Trust me, sweetheart."

Sasha has been following along on instinct thus far, waiting for Bo to tell him what to do and when, but he hadn't been quite sure what the plan was. When Bo moves to straddle David, reaching down to wrap a hand around his cock and start sinking slowly down onto it, the pieces come together in his head.

"Fuck," David swears, the first recognizable word he's said in awhile.

"*Da,*" Sasha agrees, biting his lip and doing his best not to move, to think of something else so he doesn't come in ten seconds flat. Just from watching Bo lower himself down onto David's cock, feeling the tremors roll through David's body, the way his ass clenches around Sasha's cock. Bo's weight pushes David down even further onto Sasha, a slow, sweet torture that he never wants to end.

When Bo finally settles all the way down, rotating his hips a little and making David suck in a breath, it feels like it's been a thousand years. "That good, sweetheart?" he asks, breathless again.

"Fuck," David breathes again, his fingers digging into Sasha's neck before he lets go, reaching for Bo with a trembling hand. "It's so—fuck."

"I know," Bo agrees, smirking a little. "Just wait."

And then he starts to move and all Sasha can do is hold on for the ride. With both of them on top of him, he has even less leverage than before, but it doesn't seem to matter. Bo sets a slow, almost languid pace, his face intent as he rises and falls.

"Just like that," Bo murmurs, bracing himself with one hand on David's shoulder and one hand on Sasha's. "God, look at you. You're so fucking incredible. Always so good."

"So good," Sasha agrees, grinding up into David the tiny bit he can manage, running his hands over every inch of skin he can reach. He's almost grateful that David's eyes are closed, that his back is to Sasha. If he could see their faces right now—there's no way they could hide what they feel in this moment. It's raw and intense in Bo's eyes, in the way his thumb strokes over David's collarbone. And

Sasha's never been very good at hiding his feelings so he's sure he's no better.

He's almost thankful for the overwhelming sensation, the way it fogs his brain and makes it hard to think in English. He can hear the Russian words coming out of his mouth, but that's okay. That won't scare David off before they have a chance to talk to him.

"Fuck," Bo groans, drawing what little attention Sasha has left. "I'm so close. You gonna come for us, sweetheart?"

David moans, shuddering between them. "God —please—"

"Yeah, come on," Bo says, his voice tight. "Come on, come for us, sweetheart. Want you to fill me up, just like Sash's gonna fill you up, get you all filthy. Wanna feel you—"

Sasha swears as David clenches around him, his whole body going taut with the force of his orgasm. It's enough to drag Sasha over the edge, grinding up inside David as he comes. Somewhere at the edge of his awareness he hears Bo swear, the splattering noise as he comes all over David's stomach.

And then there's nothing but the thundering of his heart where David leans back against him, as he fights to get enough air in his lungs. It would be easier, he slowly realizes, if there weren't two CHL players slumped down on top of him.

"Off," he grunts, nudging Bo's shoulder. "Can't breathe."

"Man, you ever heard of afterglow?" Bo complains, but he lifts up, wincing a little as David's cock slips free, and flops over onto the bed.

David makes an inarticulate noise, but Sasha gets an arm around his waist before he can get up, manages to roll them onto their sides. "Not yet," he says. "Is okay."

"I see how it is," Bo snarks, but he snuggles up to David's front.

"Sleep," Sasha says, letting his eyes slide closed. He's suddenly exhausted, all the physical and emotional exertion of the last few days catching up to him.

Bo huffs out a breath. "We need to clean up. No offense, babe, but I don't want to wake up stuck to you two."

"In minute," Sasha tells him.

"Fine, I'm going," Bo says, rolling out of the bed and heading toward the bathroom.

Maybe Sasha dozes off or maybe he's just drifting in a post-orgasm haze, because it seems like no time at all before Bo is back with a warm washcloth. Pulling out is just as disappointing as ever, but Sasha does it, accepts the washcloth when Bo finishes cleaning off David's front and makes sure they're both clean enough to avoid an unpleasant wakeup.

"Now sleep?" he asks plaintively, tossing the washcloth to the floor and pulling the duvet up over himself and David.

"Yeah, sleep," Bo agrees. "Nap, then dinner."

Sasha's half-asleep when he hears, as though far away, David murmur, "Was that okay?"

"That was fucking amazing," Bo replies firmly, so that's sorted out. Sasha makes an affirming noise and lets himself sink all the way down into sleep.

SASHA WAKES up in the middle of the night, unsure at first what interrupted his sleep. There's no more noise than normal, no barking dogs or car alarms. Just Bo, snoring quietly in the bed next to him—

—and that's all. David isn't there.

Sasha tries to tell himself that he probably just got up to use the bathroom, or get a drink of water. Or maybe he couldn't sleep and decided to go watch TV or game tape in the living room where he wouldn't wake them.

But Sasha's pretty sure that if he gets up and searches through the apartment, he won't find David. He's not willing to completely erase that last, fleeting hope, though. So he closes his eyes and wills himself back to sleep, tries to picture waking up with both of the men he loves in the morning.

It takes a long time before he can fall asleep again.

16

DAVID

David should be on top of the world right now. He's led his team to the playoffs. No, it's not a guarantee, but it still means a lot, especially for a team like the Wendigos. When he first got traded here, he'd assumed he'd never see another playoff run. And now here they are and as their captain, he gets to lead them into it.

He should be riding high, but instead he's slipping out from between Bo and Sasha, each movement slow and deliberate so as not to wake them, even though they both sleep heavily enough that he probably doesn't have to bother. Gathering his clothes in the dark, he sneaks out the bedroom door and closes it carefully behind him, turning the knob and releasing it slowly to keep from making a sound.

Dressing silently in the darkness of the living area, he does his best not to feel guilty. But he can't sleep, and he's pretty sure that if he stayed there, in between their two warm bodies, like they want him there—like he belongs there—he would have started fucking crying. So instead he's sneaking out the front door and locking it behind him, making his way to where Bo parked his car only a few hours ago.

There's a surprising amount of traffic on the road for four in the morning, but David's grateful. It helps distract his brain from recounting all the ways he's been stupid. And there are a lot of them.

Stupid to fall for them in the first place; what kind of asshole falls for both of his best friends? Stupid to let it show. Stupider to sleep with them, to open up his stupid, stupid heart.

Because now it's so much worse. He'd thought he was in love, before, but now? Now that he's had a taste of what it could be like, now that they've woven him into their life even more tightly than before. It's going to hurt so much worse when it ends.

So he drives through the early morning darkness. He thinks vaguely about just driving, following the road until no one can find him. But his instincts betray him, his hindbrain steering him through the familiar turns until he's pulling into his garage, walking into his house.

His empty house.

There's no way he's gotten anything like enough sleep, even though they don't have a game tonight, so he tries to lie down, to sleep again. It's not any better here, though. He keeps catching traces of Sasha's aftershave, of Bo's expensive shampoo, still lingering on the pillows. All it does is emphasize how cold and empty his bed is, no one but him breathing in the dark.

He gives up after about an hour of tossing and turning and staring at the ceiling, drags himself out of bed and pulling on shorts, a t-shirt, his running shoes. It's still not light outside, and Marian will straight-up murder him if he fucks up his ankle again, but the nervous energy under his skin won't let him be still. If he keeps it to a light jog, doesn't go too far, it should be fine.

It's hard to maintain a slow pace, he discovers as he sets out along one of his favorite routes. His body, his instincts, want him to run flat-out, to lose himself in the pounding of his feet on the pavement and his heart in his chest. To push himself until all he can think about is the next step, the next breath, the next second.

Until he can't remember what it felt like to be surrounded by Sasha and Bo, their hands on him, in him. To be trapped between their bodies and feel so, so safe. To feel Bo's body taking him in, hot and tight around him, Bo's weight pushing him down onto Sasha's cock.

To hear Bo calling him "sweetheart" like he actually cared about David as more than a friend with benefits, more than something casual.

He drags a deep, shuddering breath in through his nose, slowing down to a walk as he wipes the sweat—and other wetness—off his face. He can't outrun this. Even if he didn't have to think about the team, the season, even if he could run until he's gasping for breath and collapsed on the ground, there's no way to outrun himself.

As he turns back toward home, he forces himself to face facts. It's too late to get out of this with his heart intact—fuck, it was probably too late back before Cozumel, back before the first time Xander noticed him looking at Bo and Sasha with hearts in his eyes. All he can do at this point is mitigate the damage.

Now isn't the time to burn it all down. With the team about to go into the playoffs, the last thing they need is their captain and alternate captains at odds, or barely speaking to each other. Not that Sasha or Bo would do that; they're all fucking professionals, and they know how to keep it off the ice, out of the room.

But still.

So wait. Wait until the playoffs are over—he deliberately avoids thinking about how long that will take—and then, they'll talk. He'll explain that it's been fun, but he needs to find someone who can be a permanent part of his life. Someone he can have a relationship with. And they'll understand.

And someday David and his partner will hang out with Sasha and Bo and they'll all make jokes about how it used to be different. Hell, Bo will probably make the inappropriate joke about what David likes in bed the first time he meets this person, whoever they turn out to be. It'll be a hell of a trial by fire, but it'll be good. Really.

David swallows around the lump in his throat, the ache sitting behind his breastbone. He's got to pull it together before he sees them again. Somehow he'll have to act normal for as long as the playoffs last. As much as part of him wants to make a clean break, get it over with, another part is just fine with having a little more time with them. A few more chances, before it goes away.

He lifts up his shirt to wipe the sweat off his face.

Light.

Impact.

Pain.

Stupidly, his first thought when he goes flying is that there weren't any other players to check him.

He manages to twist so he doesn't land on his bad wrist.

Ground.

Pain.

Nothing.

17

BO

The insistent buzz of his phone on the bedside table pulls Bo rudely out of sleep. He's tempted to just ignore it, but some responsible alternate captain part of his brain has him rolling over and fumbling for it, eyes still mostly closed. "'Lo?" he mumbles, hoping he got it right side up.

"Am I speaking to Bo MacAllister?" a brisk, no-nonsense voice asks from the other end of the call. In the background he can hear beeps and buzzes and crisp sounds that all say "hospital" louder than any words.

Bo sits up all the way, adrenaline spiking like ice water down his spine. "This is he," he replies. Out of the corner of his eye, he can see Sasha sitting up too, forehead furrowed, and—where's David? Why isn't David here?

"Mr. MacAllister, my name is Kristen Gonzalez and I'm a nurse at Aurora Sinai Medical Center," the woman says, her tone somehow managing to be compassionate and matter-of-fact at the same time. "You're listed as an emergency medical contact for Mr. David Dickson?"

"Yes," Bo manages, not sure how he forces the word out through a throat gone tight. "Is he okay? Is he there? Can we—"

The nurse interrupts him. "Mr. Dickson was involved in a vehicle accident early this morning. He's not in any danger, but we are keeping him here until the doctors determine whether or not he suffered a concussion—"

"We'll be there as soon as we can—can we see him?" Bo blurts, scrambling out of bed and looking around frantically for his clothes.

"He's still in the emergency room until he's released, so you can give your name at the desk," she tells him.

Bo shoves his feet into his boxer briefs and tries to pull them up one-handed. "Thank you."

"You're very welcome," she tells him. "Good bye."

It takes him a minute to realize he's still holding the phone to his ear after the call ended, to set it down and focus on getting dressed with both hands.

"David?" Sasha asks, handing him a shirt and pulling his own over his head.

"Shit," Bo says, suddenly realizing that all Sasha has to go on is his side of the conversation. "David was in a car accident? I don't know, she didn't really give me details. He's in the ER at Aurora Sinai, they're waiting to see if he has a concussion. They called because we're the emergency contacts—shit, if we hadn't talked him into that, we wouldn't know—"

He sputters to a stop as he runs out of air, his throat closing at the idea that they wouldn't know, the mental image of David lying broken on the ground somewhere—

Sasha grabs him by the shoulders. "Breathe. He okay?"

"She said he was, but—"

"Clothes." Sasha says firmly. "Shoes. Talk more on drive."

Bo takes a shaky breath. "Right. Where the fuck are my pants?"

Somehow his pants ended up mostly under the

bed, but he finally finds them—it doesn't occur to him until he's already pulling them on that he could have just gotten another pair of pants or shorts.

"Shoes," he chants, trying to remember where he took off his shoes. He'd been so focused on David, on what they were going to do—he forcibly tears his mind away from that train of thought. By the door maybe? He heads out of the bedroom to look. There they are, sitting haphazardly by the door. He shoves his feet into them without bothering to look for socks, pats his pockets to find his keys. "Sash, you ready?"

"Got wallet?" Sasha asks, appearing out of the bedroom.

Bo reflexively checks his back pocket, but there's no wallet to be found. "Shit, where—"

"Have mine," Sasha says. "Let me drive?"

"They might need to see ID at the hospital," Bo worries. "Is it under the bed? Did it fall out when my pants ended up there?"

A quick check reveals that yes, his wallet is under the bed, and then they can go. He lets Sasha drive with only a little cajoling, even though he feels like he's about to vibrate out of his skin without something to do, because time spent arguing about it is time that they're not driving to where David is.

"Is okay," Sasha says soothingly as they wait for an opening in the early-morning traffic. "Nurse say he okay?"

"She said he's 'not in any danger.'" Bo makes possibly the most sarcastic air quotes of his life, his knee jittering up and down. "I guess they'll tell us more when we get there. But it was bad enough they're worried about concussion. Shit."

Sasha turns onto the highway, his free hand coming over to rest on Bo's knee. "But not in danger. Is good. Everything else heal."

"Yeah, but what if he wasn't?" Bo drums his fingers on the armrest. "He could've died. Whatever happened could have been worse, and he could've died, and he wouldn't have known. He wouldn't know we love him, ever. Fuck."

"That not happen," Sasha says, but his mouth is tight around the corners.

Bo knows Sasha's worried too, knows he needs to dial it back, but there's so much they don't know. They don't know how badly David's injured, other than 'not in danger,' which could mean fucking anything. They don't know if he's got a concussion —those can be career-enders, if they're bad enough. Not that Bo wouldn't love David if he never picked up a stick again, but—what chance would they have? Would he still want them around, reminders of everything he'd lost? Or would they drift apart—

"Stop," Sasha says firmly. "Whatever you thinking, stop. Will be okay. Promise."

"You don't know that," Bo retorts, because some things you never grow out of, but he reaches down and takes Sasha's hand, lacing their fingers together. "Sorry, I know. I know. I just—"

Sasha squeezes his hand back. "I know. Is hard. But David alive. That what matters."

"Yeah."

They drive in silence for a few minutes. Bo does his best not to jitter out of his seat at every traffic slowdown, every red light. He's never been more grateful for Sasha's borderline-aggressive driving style as he is right now, weaving in and out of traffic in a way that would make his heart speed up if it wasn't beating a frantic tattoo against his chest.

"We're going to tell him, right?" Bo asks as they take the exit off the freeway and turn toward the hospital. "I mean, maybe not right away, like sometimes they say that you need to keep patients calm, and this probably doesn't count. But when he's better. We tell him, playoffs or no playoffs. I can't— I can't think about missing our chance to tell him. Not again."

"*Da*," Sasha agrees, turning into the parking garage. "We tell."

Fortunately this early in the morning, it's not as packed as it might have been otherwise, but they still have to go up a couple of levels before they find a spot, the glacial pace scraping away at Bo's nerves. He's out of the truck almost before it comes to a complete stop, but Sasha's right behind him, longer legs catching up and taking his hand again.

The closer they get, the more terrified he is. As bad as not knowing is, once they find David, they'll have to deal with whatever happened. And—and they'll tell him. They need to tell him, but Bo can feel the fear that he doesn't feel the same rising up from the pit of his stomach.

He takes a deep breath and they walk through the sliding doors into the emergency department, hand in hand.

"He's very lucky," the nurse says as she leads them back through the emergency room.

Bo has to force himself to match her pace, not to run ahead—honestly the only things stopping him are Sasha's grip on his hand and the fact that he has no idea which room David is in. "So he's okay?"

"The MRIs all came back normal, but the doctor still needs to assess him for signs of a concussion," she warns, like nobody's told them that. "Other than that, the car that hit him wasn't going very fast. He's got some bruises, and a few cuts, but only one of them required stitches. He's had some pain meds, so he may be a little out of it. Don't let him fall asleep, but don't be too loud."

"We'll be quiet," Bo promises, doing his best to dredge up a winning smile. "We just want to be there with him."

She stops outside an open door. "The doctor should be with you shortly."

Sasha urges Bo through, basically pulling him along by the hand. Which is good, or Bo would've stopped in his tracks as soon as he caught side of David.

David looks—not small, exactly. He's not a small man, and being in a hospital bed doesn't change that. Vulnerable, maybe, Bo thinks, in a way that he's never seen before, not even when David was soft and asleep in their bed.

As he stands there, hesitating just inside the closed door, David blinks slowly, his eyes focusing.

"Hey," he says softly, his voice quiet. "You guys didn't have to—"

"Shut up," Bo says, only barely managing to keep from raising his voice as he crosses the room to the bed. "Of course we came. What happened?"

"Couldn't sleep. Went for a run." David's eyes start to slide closed. "Car, I think? Didn't see."

Bo reaches out to shake him, then stops, not sure how badly hurt he is. "Hey, David. Sweetheart, you have to stay awake, okay? Come on, you know the drill. Can't sleep if you might have a concussion."

"Tired," David complains, but he opens his eyes obediently.

"I know," Bo soothes. David's hands seem okay, so he takes one of them, lacing their fingers together. "Just a little longer, and we'll see what the doctor says, okay?"

He shoots a helpless look across the bed at Sasha, only getting a shrug in response. "How are you feeling?" he asks, wincing a little at the inanity of it.

"Pretty good now." David smiles beatifically. "They gave me the good drugs. Just wanna sleep."

"Soon," Sasha promises, pulling a chair up so he

can sit and keep holding David's hand. "Just wait on doctor. Want us call your parents?"

David's eyes fly all the way open at that. "Shit. No, don't call them. Not yet."

"Okay, okay, stay calm. But you should call them, after we hear what the doctor has to say."

"If my mama knows I'm in the hospital and they don't have a diagnosis yet—" David takes a deep breath through his nose. "She'll be on the next flight out. It's probably nothing."

Bo nods, does his best to keep his smile reassuring. "Yeah, probably."

Fortunately the doctor, a tall, slightly tired-looking black woman, breezes into the room before he has to come up with any more soothing platitudes. "I'm Dr. Powell. How are you feeling, Mr. Dickson?"

"Like I got hit by a car," David deadpans and Bo has to turn away to hide a completely inappropriate snicker.

"That seems right," she says, pulling up a stool. "Your MRIs were clear, no sign of brain injury. I'm just going to go over this assessment with you and then we'll release you to go home with your…?"

David blinks at her for a second, clearly not quite tracking, and the ball of worry in Bo's chest squeezes a little tighter. "Friends and teammates," Bo manages, trying not to choke on how false the words feel, how much he hates that he can't claim anything more. "We'll be with him after he goes home, keep an eye out for any further symptoms."

"Ah, that's right," she says, the pieces clearly falling into place for her. "It's been a long night, but I should've realized. My son is a huge Wendigos fan; you're his favorite, Mr. Dickson."

"Please, call me David," he manages. "And I'd be happy to sign something for him."

She shakes her head, but she's smiling. "Maybe later; I don't want to be importuning a concussion patient for an autograph. Anyway, let's get started on this. Some of these questions are ones they've already asked you. I'm going to test your memory now. I'll tell you a list of words and I want you to repeat them back to me in the same order."

Bo zones out a little bit as she goes through the concussion protocol; he doesn't take that many hits, not like the rest of the team, but there have been enough that he swears he could recite parts of it in his sleep. David does pretty well, though, he thinks. At least, the furrow on Sasha's forehead doesn't get any deeper.

"All right," the doctor says finally, sitting back.

"I don't think you're concussed, and I'm sure your friends know the drill, but I'm going to tell you anyway. If you notice any change in behavior, if the headache gets worse, nausea, vomiting, double vision, or if you can't wake him up, call your doctor right away. Tylenol and ibuprofen only for the pain unless your doctor gives you something else, alternating no more than every two hours. Complete physical rest for twenty-four hours—that means I don't want you walking any further than from the bed to the toilet or the couch, you get me?"

"Got it," Bo answers. "We'll make sure of it. Thank you, doctor."

She waves it off as she stands up. "You guys just kick some ass in the playoffs. I'll send a nurse in with the discharge paperwork."

The nurse comes back in a few minutes later, bearing paperwork and repeating the same instructions. Bo nods along and does his best to look like a person who can be trusted with an injured patient.

Then, finally, they can go. Sasha leaves to get the truck while Bo stays with David. The pain meds have mostly worn off, which is good for David's balance, but not so good for the tense way he holds himself.

Bo tells himself that's why David's so quiet as

they make their way slowly out of the emergency room and into the truck. It's because he's hurting. Not—not anything else.

He follows David into the back seat, unable to stand leaving him alone back there even for the relatively short drive, and does his best not to hover annoyingly as Sasha drives them home.

It doesn't even occur to Bo until they're ushering David through the door that they could've taken him back to his house. But it just seems right to bring him here, with them. Here to the bed he should've woken up in, safe between them.

David winces as he climbs down from the truck, but his balance still seems fine. Bo forces himself to walk a little bit ahead, not to hover like an overprotective parent. The last thing David needs right now is to be annoyed by his lack of chill.

"Tylenol?" he asks as he unlocks the door and ushers David inside, one hand lightly on the small of his back, Sasha following behind.

David nods, heading for the couch, but Bo steers him toward the bedroom door.

"You get in bed and I'll bring it to you," he

orders. "You heard the doctor. Oh, shit the sheets are still filthy. Okay, sit down on the couch while Sash and I change them, then we're taking you to the bed."

"I bet you say that to all the boys," David chirps, but it just comes out weary.

Bo exchanges a worried look with Sasha, but they have immediate priorities. It only takes a few minutes to find the clean sheets and put them on the bed. Finding the Tylenol is faster, unsurprisingly.

By the time they go back to retrieve David from the couch, he's already half asleep, blinking slowly at them.

"Come on, Sleepy," Bo says, urging him up. "Let's get you laid down, huh?"

David follows obediently, sitting down on the side of the bed. He starts to bend over to take off his shoes, but Bo gives him a dirty look and kneels down to untie them, slipping them off while Sasha hands over the Tylenol and a glass of water.

"There we go," Bo says, straightening up as David hands the empty glass back to Sasha. "Do you want your clothes off while you sleep?"

"I can take off my clothes," David says, but he winces as he reaches for the hem of his t-shirt.

Bo rolls his eyes and steps in, gently nudging his hands away and working first one arm, then the other out of the sleeves before pulling it up and over his head. "You heard what the doctor said. Do I need to call your mom and tell her you're not following medical directions?"

"No," David says sullenly.

"You don't have to do everything for yourself," Bo says softly, waiting for David to move onto the pillow before helping him off with his shorts. "We're here. We're with you. Let us help."

David submits to them pulling the covers up over him without a word, his eyes already fluttering shut again.

When Bo looks over, Sasha's already turning off the light switch, leaving the room dark except for the early morning light filtering in around the edges of the curtains. He wants nothing more than to slide under the covers with David, hold him until his hindbrain is convinced that David is real and alive and here with them.

But he doesn't even know how to hold David without hurting him right now. He reaches out to brush his fingertips over David's cheek, a barely-there touch, before turning and walking as quietly as he can toward where Sasha waits by the door.

He's reaching for the doorknob when he hears David's voice behind him, so quiet he thinks it's his imagination at first.

"I wish this was real."

Bo turns toward the bed before he realizes he's moving, sees Sasha doing the same out of the corner of his eye. He can't spare any attention for anything other than David, lying there in their bed, his eyes indescribably sad.

"I know I shouldn't be selfish. I shouldn't get in the way of what you two have. I just wish—" he starts to sit up, then collapses with a wince, obviously in pain.

"Don't hurt yourself," Bo blurts out, rushing toward the bed again. Sasha beats him there, but only by a couple of seconds. "It's okay, sweetheart, we're here, don't—don't make it worse."

David blinks up at him solemnly, but lies back obediently. "This doesn't hurt. Love hurts."

"Shouldn't," Sasha says, stroking a hand over the top of his head. "*Zvezda moya*, why love hurt?"

"Because this isn't real," David says, his eyes closing again.

Bo leans down, presses his lips to David's forehead. Gently, so gently, but firmly enough to feel. "Does that feel real?"

"Yes," David whispers.

"It's real," Bo promises. "You need to sleep, sweetheart, but—it's real. We'll talk more when you wake up."

David reaches up and grabs his hand, holding on for dear life. "Promise?"

"I promise," Bo says. "I love you. We love you."

"Really?" David's eyes fly open, even though he's clearly fighting sleep.

"Really," Sasha confirms, reaching down to take his other hand. "Sleep now, *zvezdochka.*"

It's an awkward position, but they stay like that until he sleeps so deeply that his grip on their hands finally relaxes.

18

SASHA

After the dramatic start to their morning, Sasha decides that they need a bigger breakfast than usual. He lets Bo take charge of informing the Wendigos front office of David's accident while he gets the ingredients together to make syrniki, mixing the cheese, eggs, sugar, salt, and flour together.

"Should I call his parents again?" Bo asks when he's finally off the phone, leaning against the island.

Sasha scoops flour into a bowl and closes the canister, setting it aside. "Maybe? Maybe he want to when wake up."

"Yeah." Bo drags a hand through his hair. "Hey, so, uh, sorry about like, not checking with you earlier before diving in with the L word."

"Is okay," Sasha says, stirring the cheese mixture one last time to check the consistency. "We talk before. Anyway, David need to hear."

Bo nods, his shoulders relaxing. "Yeah, I—I think so. So much for waiting for after the playoffs."

Sasha shrugs, scooping some of the cheese into the bowl of flour, coating his hands with flour and flattening it into a patty. Placing it on the waiting plate, he turns back to repeat the process.

"Holy shit, you're making syrniki?" Bo asks, finally focusing on what's happening in front of him.

"Is special day," Sasha says with another shrug. "Make special breakfast."

Bo grins at him. "You're the best Russian boyfriend I've ever had."

"Better be only Russian boyfriend," Sasha grumbles, but he knows Bo can see his smile.

DAVID EMERGES from the bedroom around the time Sasha puts the last set of syrniki into the frying pan. "Something smells good," he says hoarsely, walking slowly to the table.

"What are you doing up?" Bo exclaims,

hurrying over to hover uselessly around him as he makes his way across the room. "I was gonna bring you breakfast in bed."

"First of all, crumbs," David retorts, settling cautiously into a chair and giving Bo a skeptical look. "Secondly, I'm not broken. The doctor said I could walk short distances."

Bo sighs, sitting down in the chair next to him and reaching for his hand. "She also said complete physical rest."

"The bed was hurting my back," David says, giving him pleading eyes. "I'll lie down on the couch after breakfast, okay?"

"Fine."

Sasha carries the platter of synriki to the table where he'd already set out the applesauce, honey, jam, and sour cream in advance. He returns to the kitchen to retrieve the plate of bacon he was keeping warm in the oven, getting back to the table just in time to watch David sulkily allow Bo to put food on his plate for him.

"Glad you okay," Sasha says, squeezing the back of David's neck before settling in his own chair and serving himself.

"Me too," David says, glaring at Bo until he gets more than one strip of bacon. "But I swear I'm okay. As soon as I'm off concussion watch, I'll be out of your hair."

Sasha exchanges a confused look with Bo. "But—"

"Do you remember what we talked about before you went to sleep?" Bo asks cautiously, adding another two strips of bacon to David's plate.

David looks between them, his whole face cautiously shuttered. "I—you said—I didn't have to do everything. That you could help. You threatened to call my mom."

"I did call her after you fell asleep," Bo corrects. "Just so she wouldn't read about it on the internet. She's willing to hold off on flying out here until she's talked to you."

"Thank fuck," David mutters, dropping his eyes to his plate. "I'll call her after we eat."

He spreads jam over his syrniki and cuts off a bite. It's halfway to his mouth before Sasha realizes he's going to have to prod a little more. "Not remember anything else?"

David pauses. "I—I dreamed something else."

"Not a dream," Bo says firmly, reaching for David's free hand again. "If you mean the part where I told you I—we—love you."

The only movement is David's eyes darting back

and forth, like he's searching for confirmation. His hand is still wrapped around the fork, so Sasha settles for resting a hand on his shoulder, squeezing gently. "Is bad timing, maybe," he says quietly. "But after—well. Not want to wait more."

"I—" David takes a long, shuddering breath. "Really?"

"David Ambrose Dickson," Bo says seriously. "Sasha and I are deeply, stupidly in love with you. I was scared of fucking things up, but when I got that phone call—I don't think I've ever been more scared in my fucking life. Sash's right. I don't want to wait any longer. We want you to be with us. If—if you want that—"

David laughs, his eyes shining. "I want. Fuck, I can't remember wanting anything as much as I want that."

Sasha lets out a breath he hadn't even realized he was holding. Not that he really thought David would say no, but still. "*Khorosho,*" he says, finally turning his attention back to his plate, even if part of him doesn't want to let go of David. "Now eat. Need strength for playoffs."

"Shit," David says. "The playoffs. I—I forgot, for a minute."

"We're going to the playoffs, Captain," Bo says,

squeezing David's hand before letting go. "Better eat up."

David's smile is blinding as he obediently lifts the fork to his mouth. Under the table, he hooks a foot gently around Sasha's ankle and, judging from Bo's grin, does the same to him. "We're going to the playoffs."

They finish their breakfast like that, linked together.

"Everything looks good," Dr. Winn says, sitting back on her stool and looking at David. "No signs of concussion, and those stitches should be ready to come out in another few days. You can practice no-contact between now and then and we'll reassess at that time."

David looks stubborn, but he knows better than to argue. "What about other physical activity?"

"Skating is fine, obviously, and other cardio. No weights," she says briskly, then shoots Sasha and Bo a glance where they're sitting by the wall of the exam room. "Sex is fine as long as you're not getting too creative or athletic with it."

David ducks his head a little, and Sasha can see

Bo's cheeks going pink out of the corner of his eye. "This time of season, no creative," he says cheerfully. "Everyone too tired, sore."

"Then you should be fine," Dr. Winn says matter-of-factly. "Any other questions?"

"No," David says, still not meeting her eyes. "Thank you."

She gets to her feet, offering him a hand to shake. "No, thank *you* for actually being a patient who makes an attempt to follow directions. Don't worry, you'll be back on the ice for real soon enough."

"He's just grumpy about missing our first playoff game," Bo says cheerfully, shaking the doctor's hand when she extends it. "Don't worry, we'll make sure he takes it easy."

"I'm counting on it," she says, shaking Sasha's hand in turn before leaving the room.

David slides down from the exam table as the door closes behind her. "Let's get out of here."

"Definitely, sweetheart," Bo says, lacing their fingers together as Sasha opens the door. Thankfully for everyone's peace of mind, he waits until no one else is in earshot to add, "Can't wait to get you home and naked."

"*Da,*" Sasha agrees, holding the door for them

and following them down the hall to check out. "I drive."

They don't talk much on the drive home. It's different from the times they did this before, Sasha realizes, although the sexual tension that hangs heavy in the air is familiar. But this time, it's broad daylight, the sun shining down on them, and the air is thick with anticipation, not desperation. None of them are afraid of losing this, of damaging things beyond repair.

It's gentle, almost playful, when Bo tugs them into the apartment, pushes David back against Sasha's chest and kisses him deep and wet. Sasha keeps his touch gentle, mindful of David's injuries, when he pushes his shirt up, pulling it over his head when he and Sasha break apart.

"How do you want it, sweetheart?" Bo asks, ducking his head to kiss David's bare shoulder. "Want to make love to you, make you feel so good. Whatever you want."

David shivers between them, his hands flexing on Bo's hips. "I—can you fuck me? Both of you?"

"We can do that," Bo agrees, leaning in for another kiss. "C'mon, bedroom."

Getting to the bedroom without letting go of each other is tricky, but they manage somehow. Bo works with Sasha to strip off the rest of David's clothes and their own, the room full of the sound of kisses and soft murmurs.

"Okay, so," Bo says when they're on the bed, tangled together in a lazy, three-way makeout session that Sasha kind of never wants to end. "Do you want us to take turns? Like you and Sash did with me that one time? Or…"

"Or what?" David asks after a couple of silent moments, stroking a hand up and down Bo's arm.

Bo takes a breath. "Or we could do like that first time? I fuck you and Sash fucks me?"

"Hey," Sasha says mildly. "How come I'm only one not get fucked?"

"Because you're a fucking giant and I want to see something other than your back while we're doing this," Bo retorts, leaning over David to nip at Sasha's earlobe.

Sasha has to acknowledge the point, but he mock-pouts anyway. "Is nice back, you said."

"Very nice," David agrees, getting a handful of his ass and squeezing. "But—I think I'd like that. If you're okay with it."

"Make up to me later," Sasha agrees, leaning in to kiss David. "Promise?"

When he lifts his head, David is breathless and smiling. "Cross my heart."

"Look beautiful like this," Sasha tells him, because it's true. Because he has to say it. He's always known David was attractive; he's not blind. But like this, without the doubt and uncertainty that he hadn't recognized until it was gone? With the love he feels shining out of his face every time he looks at them?

Beautiful is the only word, even if it does make David squirm a little. "You don't have to—"

"Don't have do anything," Sasha agrees, one thumb stroking over David's cheekbone. "So beautiful, *zvezda moya*, like this."

"Like what?" David asks, his voice still a little hesitant.

It's Bo who answers, leaning in to steal his own kiss from David's lips. "Like ours."

David smiles at that, slow and gorgeous. "I am."

Sasha shifts out of the way so Bo can settle between David's legs, but he stays in touching distance, getting his own share of kisses and touches in. David gasps into his mouth as Bo's finger pushes into him, shivers under his touch as Sasha wraps a hand around his thigh and pulls it back gently, giving Bo more access. When Bo finally stops teasing, slicks up his cock and pushes slowly inside, Sasha can feel it ripple through David's body, the muscles tensing and relaxing under his hands.

"You'd better get a move on, Sash," Bo says, his voice tight as he bottoms out. "I'm not gonna last too long."

"Okay, okay," Sasha replies, stealing one last taste of David's mouth before moving behind Bo, stroking a hand down his back and reaching for the lube with the other. "So bossy, always."

Bo huffs, pulling out just a bit and thrusting back in, drawing a soft noise out of David. "Only when it's important. C'mon, babe. Want you to fuck us."

When Sasha pushes a careful finger inside, he finds Bo still loose from the last time, taking the first finger easily.

"Not gonna break," Bo tells him, ass flexing as he slowly, deliberately fucks David. "Is that all you've got?"

"Not race," Sasha tells him, but he adds more lube, another finger, scissoring them apart.

David laughs, his face fond as he looks up at Bo, then meets Sasha's eyes. "I don't know, man. I'm not gonna—fuck—last long either."

"Fine," Sasha agrees, withdrawing his fingers and slicking his cock. "He fuck you good?"

"So good," David says, the last word going soft and breathy as he reaches up to wrap his hands around Bo's arms. "Fuck, it's so good. Want you, too. C'mon, Sasha, fuck us."

Sasha lines himself up and starts pushing inside by way of answer. His arousal, easy to ignore while making out or working Bo open, suddenly pushes to the forefront with the hot, slick, tight clasp of Bo's body around his cock, the little unconscious noises both David and Bo are making with each tiny thrust it takes to work himself inside. He's panting by the time he's fully seated, hanging onto control by his fingernails, his hands shaking on Bo's hip, on David's arm.

"Fuck," Bo says softly, his hips moving in little hitching grinds, trying to get Sasha even deeper. "Oh, fuck, Sash—"

"Need minute?" Sasha asks hoarsely. Every cell in his body is screaming at him to move, to thrust, to come.

Bo nods. "Yeah, I—just a minute."

"Fuck," David says, blinking his eyes open and looking up at them wonderingly. "I—"

"Yeah," Bo agrees shakily. "I don't know how you didn't come on the spot, that first time."

David smiles ruefully. "Almost did. But this—"

"I know." Bo shifts his hips experimentally, drawing groans out of David and Sasha both. "Okay, I think—yeah, go for it."

Sasha keeps his first thrust small, just a tiny withdrawal and push back in, rocking Bo deeper into David, but it draws breathy little noises from both of them.

"Fuck," David moans, his eyes fluttering shut as Sasha moves again. "Fuck, if I watch that, I'm gonna come in like, a second. You're—shit, you're—"

"Yours," Bo says, his voice equally breathless. "We're yours."

David moans again at the words, his fingers digging into Bo's arms. "Oh, fuck."

"Yours," Sasha agrees, doing his best to keep his thrusts slow and measured. "Love you, *zvedochka*."

"Love you," Bo echoes, getting a hand between them to wrap around David's cock. "C'mon, sweetheart, let us see you. Always so gorgeous when you come for us."

Sasha picks up the pace a little, matching Bo's

strokes, touching both of them wherever he can reach. It's only a few moments before David comes with a soft cry. It sets off a chain reaction, Bo coming almost immediately after, his body tightening around Sasha until he can't hold off his own orgasm any longer.

He barely retains enough presence of mind not to just collapse on top of them, but it's a near thing, sucking in air as his racing heart slowly calms. He needs to get up, he knows, get something for them to clean up with or coax them into the shower. Eventually he'd like to lie down, maybe take a nap with Bo and David cuddled in bed with him. But for now, they're together, bodies entangled, skin on skin, and he can't think of anything else he wants, anywhere else he wants to be.

"I love you," David says, his voice quiet but unmistakable. When Sasha blinks his eyes open, David is looking right at him, then at Bo, his face soft and open. "Both of you."

"Love you," Sasha echoes, Bo repeating it a few seconds behind.

No, there's nowhere he'd rather be.

19

DAVID

"Okay," David says to the locker room, taking a moment to meet each set of eyes. They're all exhausted, Jordan and Marian moving around quietly applying ice packs and kinesio tape. He doesn't have the energy to raise his voice, but he doesn't really need to. They're all listening, conserving their energy as much as possible.

"It's game seven. We have twenty minutes left. We need one goal. I know you're tired, and hurting. But I need you to give me more. I need, we need, everything you have. I'm not asking for twenty minutes. I'm asking for one second, and then another one, where you give it everything you've got."

It's not so much a murmur of agreement as a quiet roar, the energy zipping from person to person until David can feel it sizzling under his skin. He glances at Sasha, at Bo. It's not as good a touch, but even if they weren't all geared up, he doesn't think he could muster up the energy to move to where they are.

He sits in his stall and does his best to force down the Gatorade he knows he needs, lets Marian lift the ice pack off his wrist when she gets to him.

"How is it?" she asks quietly, her fingers gently probing around the bones before moving down to the knee he sprained in game three, repeating the process.

"No worse," he says honestly, meeting her eyes steadily.

She finally sighs, putting the ice pack back down and handing him a couple of ibuprofen. "I'm telling Sasha to carry you everywhere for a week after this is over."

"He'd probably like that," David agrees with a smile, taking the pills and washing them down with the last of his Gatorade.

And then their time is up. David forces himself up off the bench, takes his place at the door as the rest of the team files out. He doesn't say anything;

there's nothing left to say. But he offers a fistbump or a backslap for each of his teammates, peripherally aware of Sasha on the other side.

Ads is the last one out, leaving him alone with Bo and Sasha, except for the staff. He nods to Sasha and they clomp down the tunnel toward the arena, Bo behind them, the roar of the crowd rising higher with each team member who takes the ice or slides onto the bench.

"Love you," David breathes as they move onto the ice together, almost too quiet to be heard under the noise. But he sees the return look from both of them, sees their lips move in response as they separate, Bo to the goal, Sasha to his position, David meeting the Sirens center for the face-off.

He's smiling when the puck hits the ice.

THAT STRANGE CALM stays with him throughout the period, as the seconds tick down without a point for either side. Bo stops everything that comes toward him, a solid wall of denial, but Marsh, the Sirens goalie is just as good, and nothing is getting through.

Three minutes and change left on the clock

when White sends their line out again, David and Sasha going over the boards at the same time, Xander, Becks and Elvis a split second behind them. The Sirens defense is on them almost instantly, but David fakes around them, laser focused on the puck. Trusting Sasha to have his back.

Sasha snakes the puck from someone in a gold jersey and passes it to David who takes off for the goal, pouring every last bit of energy into his aching legs. Every instinct he has says this is it, this is his chance. In his peripheral vision, he can see Sasha clearing a path for him, keeping the Sirens off him as he claws his way closer and closer—

The opening comes and he reacts on instinct, slapping the puck with all the force he can muster, watching it fly toward the goal faster than he can skate. Marsh lunges, deflecting it—

—directly back toward him—

—Marsh overbalances, goes sprawling across the ice—

—David puts on a last burst of speed he didn't think he had in him, gets his stick on the puck, and knocks it into the goal.

The entire arena erupts as the goal horn sounds. Sasha's the first one to crash into him, but Xander and Becks hit them almost at the same time, Elvis joining in. David manages to twist so he hits the ice on his ass, not his knee, his heart racing, adrenaline pumping. "Get off me, assholes," he laughs breathlessly. "We still have a minute."

It's bullshit and they know it. They can feel the momentum shifting as they skate back to center ice, as they settle in for the face-off, even when the Sirens pull Marsh. Snaking the puck from the Sirens center feels like the easiest thing David's ever done, even when he has to pass to Becks almost immediately.

They thread their way through the Sirens, passing the puck back and forth. David takes a hip check that makes a sudden, stabbing pain shoot through his knee. But seconds later, Elvis knocks the puck into the empty net, the sweet sound of the goal horn, the cheers of the crowd and his team making him laugh out loud.

David can practically see the energy seeping out of the Sirens as the final seconds count down. Oh, they keep trying, but they know, everyone knows, that the Wendigos have won.

He turns to Sasha as soon as the final buzzer sounds, throwing his helmet to the ice and all but leaping into his arms, screaming incoherently. Their momentum carries them toward the goal, where Bo has ripped off his mask and is skating toward them, crashing into them.

The rest of the team is headed for them, the ones on the bench pouring over the boards, but all David can see is the two men he loves. "I love you," he yells, loud enough to be heard in the nosebleeds, and drags Sasha in for a fierce, filthy kiss, before doing the same to Bo. "God, I fucking love you!"

Whatever reply they make is lost in the pile as the rest of the team joins them, but that's all right.

He knows.

ACKNOWLEDGMENTS

So many people were a support on this project that I'm honestly a little scared I'll forget to thank someone, but here goes! Big thank you to Liz and Foz for being my first readers and helping me figure out where this story was even going. To the OMGCP Discord for squeeing over *Soft Hands* and being excited for David, Bo, and Sasha's story. To my Patreon supporters for putting their money where their mouth is; I hope you know how much it means to me. To Ant and Jamesiee for the super quick last-minute typo check—seriously, I owe you big time. To Dresupi, Pink, and Cherie for always being there for venting and rubber-ducking as necessary.

To everyone who bought *Soft Hands*, you may

never know what it meant to me. Just the fact that people would pay to read what I had written was a much-needed ray of light in a very dark time. You gave me hope that I could escape a toxic situation and motivation to keep putting words on paper.

And, always and forever, more thanks than I can say to Alex and Brittany, for believing in me, supporting me, putting up with at best half of my attention while I wrote and edited, for listening to me whine, understanding when I needed writing time, and just generally being amazing partners. I love you.

ABOUT THE AUTHOR

Ariel Bishop is an American romance and erotica author who feels strongly that all love triangles are best resolved through healthy polyamory. She lives in the Ozarks with her partners, their children and two bunnies that rejoice in the names Reginald von Pancakes and Snickers.

More information about her books can be found at her website or by signing up for her mailing list, and you can chat with her directly in her Facebook Group. You can also find her on Tumblr, Twitter, and Facebook. For sneak previews of upcoming books in the Tripping series and other rewards, you can support her on Patreon.

Keep reading for a list of her other works and a sneak peek at book 3 in the Tripping series, *Holding!*

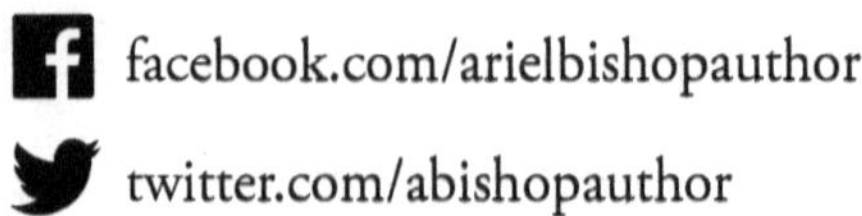

facebook.com/arielbishopauthor

twitter.com/abishopauthor

UNTITLED

Enjoy this sneak peek at Holding, Book 3 in the Tripping series, coming in October 2018!

Tolya

Michaelson and Petrov Bond On and Off the Ice

Kevin Michaelson and Anatoly Petrov aren't your usual CHL rookies. At 21, with three seasons of NCAA hockey under his belt, Michaelson is understandably more mature than the average 18-year-old prospect fresh out of the draft. And while Petrov was one of those 18-year-olds, being Vladislav Petrov's son didn't keep him from doing his time in the minors.

"It's a little different," Michaelson agrees when asked about it. "I mean, it's exciting, for sure. But this isn't my first time living on my own. I'm glad Tolly's here, otherwise it would be a little weird, just me and the other rookies. I'd feel a little creepy, to be honest."

Petrov nods. "Mikey's a good roommate."

It's clear after spending even a few minutes with them that their friendship is not just a product of the Abs' PR team. Both of them are very comfortable with each other, laughing at least twice at inside jokes that they can't really seem to explain beyond "you had to be there."

But as much as the fans love their friendship, their on-ice chemistry is what has people excited to see what happens this season. Both Petrov and Michaelson are quick to say that it's a team effort, of course, but there's no denying that they're putting up some impressive point totals for their rookie season, particularly

Michaelson, with three points in his first regular season game.

"There's still a lot of season left," he says, ducking his head bashfully. "We're just trying to take it one game at a time."

"Okay," Stewie says, looking around the locker room, his captain face firmly in place. "You know what to do. Let's go out there and get it done."

Tolya adds his voice to the wordless roar of assent, stands with the rest of the team to file out of the locker room. The familiar ball of nerves and anticipation is tight in his stomach, even months into the season. He suspects it won't ever completely go away, isn't entirely sure he wants it to. He'll have to ask his father the next time he's home.

But right now, with Mikey a comforting presence behind him, accepting a fist bump from his captain as he files down the tunnel and joins most of the team on the bench, everything is good. The Wendigos are having a pretty good season, but so are the Abs. Tolya can practically taste the anticipation in the air, feel it in the way Mikey's shoulder bumps into his as they lean forward to watch the face-off.

It's a good game, the kind of game Tolya loves to watch. Not too chippy, lots of skill on the ice. The Wendigos are faster than he remembers from last season, and they score in the first, their goalie somehow managing to stop all the Abs' shots on goal. Still, it's just the first period. Even when it ends without them getting an answering goal, the mood is still good as they head back to the locker room.

"Man, MacAllister's on fire tonight," Mikey mutters, rubbing a towel over his hair. It stands up in dark clumps that make Tolya's fingers itch to smooth them back down.

"We've got two more periods," he says instead. "Just gotta keep it together."

Mikey rolls his eyes. "Thanks, Coach."

Tolya shrugs. "You know it's true."

"Yeah," Mikey sighs. "I know."

"Cheer up," Tolya says, bumping their knees together. "I'm buying tonight."

Mikey grins crookedly. "Well, then. Let's light it up."

AS THE MINUTES tick down on the second period, Tolya can feel the mood shift, the certainty of defeat creeping in even though no one says anything. When Hartsburg scores again for the Wendigos, it's like a shockwave going through the team. Being down 0 and 2 isn't a death sentence, but it's starting to feel like one.

With only a couple of minutes left to go, Coach Daniels waves their line over the boards. Tolya shoves his mouthguard back between his teeth and obeys, Mikey at his side like they share the same brain. He does his best to wipe everything from his head, to just get to the puck. The Wendigos are tired, too—if he's going to have a chance, this is as good a time as any.

He's so focused on the puck that he almost doesn't see it begin. The sudden motion of Plats falling in the corner of his eye catches his attention, and his head whips around just in time to see the Wendigo d-men barely avoid him, almost colliding as they deke around to keep their skates away from his fallen body.

But there's no way for Mikey to avoid him. Tolya watches in horror as Mikey tries to jump, his skates catching on a rough spot in the ice. As Mikey goes flying through the air. As Mikey hits the ice with an audible crack, his whole body going limp, his arm bent at a terrible, unnatural angle that turns Tolya's stomach.

He doesn't even realize he's moving until it's already happened. He's too late, he knows he's too late, but he can't stop himself, sliding the last few meters on his knees so he doesn't collide with Mikey's still, broken body. It's wrong, so wrong, for Mikey to be so still. Mikey's never still, even in his sleep, some part of him always moving. But he's still now, and Tolya can feel the dread rising up in his throat like vomit.

"You've got to let us through, son," someone says, kindly but firmly, from behind him.

Tolya turns his head to see the medics. That's good. He shifts back enough to let them work, struggles to his feet. When the woman checking Mikey's pulse nods to her colleague, it feels like the first time he's breathed in hours.

But that relief is short-lived. He keeps waiting, waiting for Mikey to open his eyes, to smile and crack a joke. To be okay, like he was just a minute ago. But the medics slide a board under him, lift him carefully onto the stretcher. Tolya has to bite back a protest when they strap him down; Mikey would hate that.

Then they're wheeling him off the ice, the arena silent as they watch. Tolya takes a breath, then another, tries to get himself back mentally to where he should be. It's the game. He knows this, down to his bones. He has to be ready, to play. No matter what.

It's a shameful relief when the officials call the period, when he can file back down the tunnel and into the locker room.

That intermission, with Mikey's stall empty beside him, is the longest one of Tolya's life.